Proper Suda

Proper Suda

a novel

Mike Whicker

a Walküre book

Proper Suda

a Walküre imprint
email: walkure@mikewhicker.com

This is a work of historical fiction.

ISBN: 978-0-9844160-4-2

Printed in the United States of America

Forward

Scheherazade, the spellbinding storyteller of *Arabian Nights,* shows us the power of stories; her stories saved her life. It has been said that humans need stories as much as they need food and water. We know this is true. Scheherazade, like Homer, told stories in the oral tradition. We still do this today, plus we use books, movies, and television to supply our stories. Even when we daydream, we tell ourselves a story. We have to have them.

Our story is the result of a project conducted in my classrooms during the 2002-2003 school year at F.J. Reitz High School in Evansville, Indiana. Research allowed us to do the following:

During the fall semester, the F.J. Scribes and I traveled back to the Evansville of 1921 and met a remarkable yet enigmatic young lady with the strange name of Suda. We strolled the streets and neighborhoods of that Evansville of long ago and sat in on some classes at Reitz—a brand new school in those days. When we returned to 2002, as fate (and imagination) would have it, a football player at our school stumbled upon a diary written by Suda. We had no choice but to pursue the story.

In the spring, students in my creative writing class helped revise and edit the story until we had our novel.

The F.J. Scribes conducted research, studied and practiced narrative and dialogue writing techniques, worked on character development, and suggested and labored on scenes and plot. Surely the students learned the importance and value of revising and editing written work not once, but many times.

We were forced to make some decisions. Some suggested Suda's comments concerning certain ethnic groups, especially Native Americans, are too abrasive. This topic stoked some lively debate among the F.J. Scribes. After much discussion, we refused to censor Suda. We resisted the omnipresent shadow of political correctness for the sake of historical setting and character development. Like all of us, Suda must learn of the pitfalls of stereotyping.

Some Scribes suggested the use of names of real life Reitz teachers in the story. Others thought this unfair if not all were mentioned. Using the names of ninety teachers would be impossible, of course. As with the political correctness issue, this was another consideration that the

F.J. Scribes took seriously. The Scribes decided that if the character portrayed a single position: one counselor's secretary, one principal, one head football coach, one Media specialist, then borrowing an actual name would be acceptable if permission was granted. In the case of teachers and assistant football coaches, where everyone's name could not possibly be used, fictitious names were decided upon.

Amid all these heavy debates, we never lost track of one of our first rules: to not take ourselves too seriously. We had fun visiting Suda and Tommy in 1921, and hanging out in the present with Joe and Morgan.

There is a saying in Hollywood: "Never let the truth, or history, get in the way of a good story." But the Scribes invested a great deal of time researching the 1920s Ku Klux Klan and the infamous D.C. Stephenson. We learned of Joe Huffington and the Horse Thief Protection Agency, and the weighty influence the Klan wielded in Evansville during Suda's time. Great effort was made to stay true to history—the Scribes studied the importance of verisimilitude, and the rules that govern a reader's suspension of disbelief. So we will argue that our story is very respectful of history. Details such as the Meyer's Drug Store soda fountain being a popular place for teenagers to go in 1921, the address of the Klan headquarters in 1921 Evansville, and even details concerning immigrant processing at Ellis Island were researched by the students before being incorporated into the story. The Westside Nut Club was contacted for information about the first Fall Festival, which by coincidence was held in 1921. However, even with the great deal of time and leg work invested in historical research, we can never forget that when writing a novel our first responsibility is the same one that guided Scheherazade—to tell a story.

Our work is fiction.

And in the end, we consider it just a simple tale of high school football, past and present.

Mike Whicker
May 2003

Acknowledgments

How can we thank Amy Walker, Dr. Charles F. Harrington, and the entire staff of the Public Education Foundation of Evansville? All we can say is without the PEF's generous grant this project would have never seen the light of day.

We owe our gratitude to F.J. Reitz High School principal Christine Settle, and English department chair, Beth Edwards. They stand bravely against the dragon of public education budget woes and fight the battle to continue offering quality elective classes to students—like the Reitz creative writing class that helped with various aspects of this story.

Bob Hammonds of the Reitz Media Center and Pam Locker of the Red Bank Library expertly and efficiently steered us through much of our research. Another thanks is due Pam, who read a rough draft of our story and offered her insight.

Concerning the 1920s Ku Klux Klan, Jean Berger and Jon Carl supplied us with so much detailed information our tale probably does not do their help justice. If there are any historical inaccuracies concerning the Klan during Suda's time, they are surely not the fault of Jean or Jon. In addition, Jon, along with Dick Barchet, supplied us with some hard to find information about the history of the Westside Nut Club Fall Festival.

No author can have too many proofreaders. Beside the F.J. Scribes, Professor Eric Vonfuhrmann, Paula Harmon, Nicole Stucki, and Beth Carnahan offered this invaluable service.

To Terry Hughes and Karen McBride of the EVSC iCats: thank you.

Paige L. Dodson created our cover artwork. Thanks, Paige.

Judy Neff at the Evansville Catholic Diocese has to be thanked for the valuable research she did for us.

Tom Egan, a true heavyweight in the wonderful world of books, has supported this project since its inception. We are much obliged, Tom.

And luck was with us when Dr. Susanna Hoeness-Krupsaw agreed to proofread the manuscript and offer suggestions. Having her name on our back cover lends considerable weight to our project.

The F.J. Scribes

The F.J. Scribes were students at F.J. Reitz High School in Evansville, Indiana, during the 2002-2003 school year. These students worked on *Proper Suda* in at least one of the following capacities: research, scene and story practice and development, character development, revision suggestions, and/or editing suggestions.

Alphabetical Order:

Andrew Angel
Angela Arnold
Nick Basham
Anna Becher
Alison Blikken
Elaine Bigge
Joshua Boardman
Crystal Boatman
Ashley Brown
Kendra Browning
Brett Bunner
Erica Bush
Emily Carrico
Brent Casper
Darryl Chamberlain
Chad Cook
Lesley Corbett
Andy Deig
Amanda Fehrenbacher
Corissa Haas
Joshua Hart
Billy Hazelton
Drew Helfert
Aaron Henze
Zach Hermann
Sara Hertweck
Leslie Hoppel
Brent Hunter
Joe Hurley
Michael Hurley
Jennifer Johnson
Tamara Johnson
Andy Kissel
Adam Lauer
Adam Lentz
Lauren Little
Mark Lovelace
Sean Martin
Chad Offerman
Robyn Orth
Jeff Owens
Nickie Peak
Adrian Randolph
Megan Reed
Matt Riecken
Stephen Rogers
Brian Roy
Katherine Schonberger
Janelle Seib
Jeremy Simon
Laura Tenbarge
Candice Thomas
Zach Tieken
Brittany Tyler
Devin Vaught
Kelli Whicker

Cover artwork by
Paige L. Dodson

For my grandchildren
Those born and those still waiting

Chapter 1

It was August.

And it was the first game of the season. Number 50 stood by the door of the fieldhouse, sweat dripping from eyebrows under a shining silver helmet. Kickoff was fifteen minutes away, but already perspiration soaked the T-shirt under his shoulder pads. Number 50 knew the sweat had little to do with the weather. While August in southern Indiana with its heat and humidity rivals the Congo, number 50 always sweated profusely before a game, even before late season games when the weather might be bitter cold. The rigorous pregame warm up and stretch routine Coach Hart put his team through brought on the sweat (that, but especially nerves).

As far back as pee wee football, number 50 had been forced to deal with nasty pregame nerves. Last year, his junior season, he had finally found a way to control the vomiting. He quit eating the day of the game (till after the game when he and some friends would invade Steak-n-Shake). No eating before the game and a half bottle of Pepto Bismol usually kept him from coughing up his spleen on the thirty yard line during pregame warm up.

Every player on the team had his own way of preparing for games. Some guys had to have a massive dose of hard and loud rap or heavy metal blasting through their CD headsets. Others demanded quiet. Lucky wrist bands, lucky T-shirts, and lucky chinstraps were everywhere. Tim Grainger, the six-foot-five tight end, claimed the ghost of Marilyn Monroe came to him in a dream one night his sophomore year warning him to always carry a picture of her with him during the games. Every game since then a picture of Marilyn had been taped inside the cantilever of his shoulder pads.

Even many of the coaches had strange pregame rituals. One of the defensive coaches had a lucky pair of game socks, one brown, one black. The brown must be worn on the left foot, or was it the right? Coach

Hart, the head coach, had for years polished his shoes the day of the game in a detailed manner—the specifics were as top secret as anything in the playbook.

But number 50 did not believe much in superstitions—just make sure the bottle of pink stuff was on hand along with a bottle of ibuprofen to help with post game soreness.

The fieldhouse stood north of the stadium which was an amphitheater structure carved into the side of a hill. It was one of the largest high school football stadiums in Indiana. Number 50 knew how lucky he was to play football for Reitz High School; the Evansville school has, for generations, been one of the premier prep football programs in the state. Number 50's dad had worn the silver helmet, so had his grandfather (actually his grandfather's helmet was leather with no face mask).

Reitz Bowl could accommodate twelve thousand fans. Looking out from the fieldhouse doorway, number 50 estimated the stands to be half-filled, with people still entering. A great crowd would be on hand for the season opener. Suddenly, he heard the cue from Coach Hart who had stepped out of the coaches' office.

"Captains, take 'em out!"

Number 50, along with the three other team captains, began the short walk to the field accompanied by the cacophony of football cleats clicking and scrapping on concrete steps—the sound like hail hitting a tin roof. The opposing team was already on their sideline when the home crowd spotted their team emerging from the fieldhouse. The crowd rose to its feet and loudly greeted the team as cheerleaders rocketed skyward—thrown high and then caught by their cheermates. Clouds of moths barnstormed each set of stadium lights. As was tradition, the team gathered under the north goalpost then ran to the middle of the field. After they moved to the sideline, the team formed a human tunnel for the players who would be introduced. Tonight it was the defense's turn. The familiar voice of Craig Prindle, the PA announcer, cracked through the speakers. Number 50 waited as the linemen were introduced, then Prindle called out the names of the linebackers.

"At outside linebacker, number 44, Rick Turner!" The crowd yelled and Turner sprinted through the tunnel of teammates who vigorously slapped and pounded his helmet and shoulder pads.

"At outside linebacker, number 38, Greg Hillyard." Hillyard held a clenched fist high and took his turn fighting his way through the gauntlet of excited teammates.

"At middle linebacker, number 50, Joe Rocker!"

"How can you eat all that crap?"

Rick Turner asked this question of Joe Rocker as they sat in a booth at Steak-n-Shake. With the two football players was Rick's girlfriend, Becky Taylor. A visit to the Steak-n-Shake was a required post game custom for many members of the team. The restaurant was loud with teenagers. A matted up napkin, thrown by a teammate two booths away, narrowly missed Turner.

"Mind your own business," Joe said as he took a huge bite out of his third double cheeseburger. "I haven't eaten all day." Joe then turned up a large glass and drank his second chocolate milkshake.

"Yeah, mind your own business," Becky nudged Rick. "Besides, you don't exactly eat like Ghandi yourself: Mr. Pattie Melt, double order of onion rings, and bowl-of-chili man." Becky made a sour face that made Joe laugh.

"Well, I don't make a disgusting spectacle out of myself like our boy here," Rick pressed his case as he watched Joe stuff French fries into his already full mouth.

It was good-natured kidding between friends for it was a good night. The game had gone well. Reitz won by ten points (it could have been much more if the offense had not sputtered badly during the first half) and there were no serious injuries. Turner had escaped with only a ripped fingernail and a few bruises on his forearms. Joe Rocker had a lump on a shin and a cut on his nose. All the injuries were normal, everyday stuff for football players, injuries that would heal quickly. As long as they didn't keep a player out of practice and next week's game—that's all that mattered.

And for Joe, the sliced-open nose was well worth it. It was the result of the bridge of his helmet jamming down on his nose when he delivered a tremendous hit on the enemy fullback. It was third and two but Joe stuffed the fullback at the line for no gain with one of those big hits that football players dream about and crowds "Ooh!" Those hits Joe Rocker loved and they were his trademark. He had always been what football coaches call "a hitter." He proved as much his sophomore year when he made several spectacular hits on special teams early in the season. Mid-season of Joe's sophomore year an injury sidelined the senior playing middle linebacker and the coaches decided, because of his hustle in practice and play on special teams, to try Joe at middle linebacker over another senior and a couple of juniors who played the position. The senior Joe replaced was ready to return three games later, but by then Joe had proved to the coaches that he was their guy. The senior never got his position back. Since then Joe Rocker had been the starting varsity middle linebacker. People commented that his last name fit his style of play and Joe took pride in that. He had seen the "Time to Rock 'em!" and "Are You Ready to Get Rocked?" signs students held up in the stands.

When it became time to call it a night, the boys paid the bill and everyone loaded into Rick's pickup truck. Becky squeezed into the middle. Rick let Joe out in front of his house.

"Good night, Joe," Becky said. "Good game."

"See ya later," Joe said.

It was still warm and humid, even now at midnight. Joe Rocker was happy with the way he played in this first game of his senior season. He was hoping to earn a football scholarship to college, and he was already getting mail from some college coaches who said they would be watching him this season. At 6'1" and 220 pounds he had adequate height for his position and he would gain weight in college. Size was not his problem. His Achilles heel was a 4.8 second forty yard dash. That was a good enough time for a high school middle linebacker, but not for a college linebacker. And that was his ultimate goal—a college football scholarship. Joe knew he would have to lower that forty yard dash time if he expected to impress the college coaches.

As Joe walked up the driveway to his home, a sudden impulse stirred him. He jumped in his dad's pickup (his dad gave him a key and paid for his insurance during football season—the rest of the year Joe was responsible for his insurance). Joe drove to Reitz Bowl, parked the truck, and hopped the fence. The lights were black and the crowd gone. In a half-moon's light, Joe could see the trash from that night's game littering the concrete stands.

Some believed Reitz Bowl was haunted. There was a legend that the ghosts of great players and coaches long dead visited the stadium at midnight on game nights during the fall. The phantasms were assembled to recall glorious deeds past and to play a ghostly game on the hallowed turf of the revered stadium.

But these ghostly visits were allowed only when the present day team won.

In the dark, Joe Rocker walked out to mid-field and stood looking for the spectral game.

"We won tonight, boys. You can come out now."

It was said tongue-in-cheek.

Joe Rocker did not believe in ghosts.

Chapter 2

"Grab me one of those four-inch quarter bends, Joe."

Joe Rocker put down his shovel and sorted through a stack of cast-iron sewer fittings until he found the one his father needed. Joe's father owned a plumbing business and Joe had worked at the family business in his spare time since his middle school days. Joe knew about four-inch quarter bends. He pulled one from the stack of fittings and handed it to his father.

They were replacing the underground sections of a sewer line for a house on Stinson Avenue. During football season Joe's spare time was very limited, and he seldom worked with his father until the playoffs ended sometime in November. But today was Sunday, Joe's only day off from football, and he decided to help out. The digging would keep him loose, and he could use the money. His dad gave him a small allowance during football season, but it was barely enough to pay for the enormous Friday night meals at Steak-n-Shake. So Joe worked Sundays when his dad was busy.

Joe's father inserted the last section of pipe and sealed it with a rubber gasket. "I'm sure glad we don't have to lead the joints anymore—like in the old days. Check the drop on this section, Joe, then we're ready for the inspectors."

With a four foot level, Joe checked to make sure there was a quarter of an inch drop for every foot of sewer pipe.

"Looks okay."

"Good, go ahead and gather the tools. I'll tell the homeowners they can now use the water and that we'll call for inspection tomorrow."

During the drive home, their conversation focused mostly on the team's chances on the gridiron.

"You played a good game the other night. You guys look like you'll be pretty tough this year."

"Thanks, Dad. Yeah, if we can get the offense going we should do okay."

"The guys at the VFW keep asking me when Coach is going to liven up his play calling a little. Frank Harper keeps telling everyone about his son's rocket arm." Joe's dad had served in Vietnam and was a regular at the west side VFW Post. Frank Harper's son, Kevin, had taken over as the team's starting quarterback after last year's All-City quarterback, Ryan Braun, graduated.

"I'll be sure and give that scouting report to Coach Hart," Joe said. They both laughed.

"How's school? Do you like your teachers?"

"They're okay. I think I told you I have Coach Lee for English." Joe's dad nodded. Coach Lee taught senior English at Reitz and was the longtime freshman football coach. Joe played for Coach Lee when he was a freshman. Coach Lee was known far and wide for his corny jokes, shiny bald head, disheveled appearance, and a complete lack of taste when it came to neckties—his favorite featuring the Three Stooges.

"One day last week," Joe continued, "Coach Lee gave us an in-class reading assignment. The room was real quiet when all of a sudden Coach Lee's stomach started to growl. It was real loud and grossed out the girls, but the guys started laughing. Coach Lee seemed embarrassed and tried to tell us the sound was coming from the radiator. He even went over and kicked it a couple of times. That just made everyone crack up more. He finally had to admit he was the source of the noise, but then he blamed it on a cafeteria burrito."

Joe's dad chuckled and shook his head. They were now home and as Mr. Rocker turned the truck into the driveway he changed the subject back to business.

"Next week I start an extensive remodeling job on that property I bought on Wabash Avenue. You know that big, 125-year-old house I told you about." Joe nodded and his father continued. "First I have to tear out before I can fix up the place. I can use some help again next Sunday if you want to make a few bucks."

"Sure, Dad."

The answer was perfunctory, given without thought. Little did Joe Rocker know at the time that working that next Sunday on an old house on Wabash Avenue would be a day he would remember forever.

[One Week Later]

"This closet wall has to come down," Mr. Rocker told Joe, "then we'll clean up and head home. I'll grill you a T-bone. How's that sound?"

"Sounds good, Dad."

For the past four hours, Joe Rocker had torn pipes from ceilings, electrical wiring from walls, and ripped drywall, plaster, and trim from the top floor of a large, 19th century home on Wabash Avenue. Once a showcase, in recent years the house had fallen into disrepair. The last owner, an attorney who purchased the property for a tax write-off, turned the historic old mansion into efficiency apartments and rented them out to college students who, with great efficiency, reduced the structure to little more than a slum. The attorney got his write-off but decided to sell the property to avoid the negative publicity when a neighborhood historical society got up in arms about the demise of the once beautiful old home. Joe's father got a bargain and planned to restore the house to a single family home (a goal that pleased the historical society to no end).

The closet wall Joe's father referred to was in a bedroom on the top floor at the rear of the house. The walls were not drywall, which was easy to rip out. Instead, they were thick plaster and it took Joe several swings of a sledge hammer to make a hole large enough to finish the work with a reciprocating saw. Joe removed sections of the wall two stud spacings wide and threw the plaster out an open window into the backyard.

It was not unusual to find interesting artifacts when working on old homes. Last summer, in an attic, Joe came across a collection of yellowed newspapers almost a hundred years old. Earlier that day, Joe's father found an old soft drink bottle in the cellar with an image of Babe

Ruth on it and the words *"The Bambino loves Orange Crush."* Clearly, because the claim was made in the present tense, the Babe was still playing baseball when the bottle was manufactured.

As Joe removed the last section of plaster, he noticed something resting between what a moment ago was a wall and the plywood sheathing attached to the other side of the studs. Joe picked it up and blew off the dust of ages. He held what looked to be an old towel wrapped around something and tied with a string. Joe untied the twine that still had a perfect bow and removed the cloth. Inside was a leather bound book of some kind. Joe opened the book, probably too roughly, and the spine cracked.

He turned to the front page of the book and read the handwritten words:

Diary of Suda Mae Jackson.

Joe almost threw the diary out the window with the last of the plaster, but he decided if it contained anything historical it might earn him a few extra credit points in history class.

Joe tossed the diary into his toolbox.

Chapter 3

Joe Rocker was tired and ready for bed.

It had been a grueling practice that Wednesday afternoon. Coach Hart had gotten upset at some of the guys messing around in the lockerroom before practice and made the entire team run the stadium steps for twenty minutes *before* practice began.

Joe was starting up the stairs to his room when he heard his mother call. He found her in the dining room.

"Joe, be a dear and hang this picture for me." His mother held a framed family photograph on the wall to show him where to hang it.

"I'm dogged out, Mom."

"It'll just take you a minute. And when you're done, don't forget to take your laundry up to your room."

Joe needed a Phillips screwdriver so he went out into the garage where he kept his toolbox. He had completely forgotten about the old diary he had found last weekend in the house on Wabash Avenue, but when he opened the lid of the toolbox, there it was. He grabbed the diary, along with the screwdriver, and went back into the house. He threw the diary on the stack of clean laundry. After hanging the picture, a tired Joe Rocker lugged his laundry up to his room.

Ready for bed, Joe reached over to flip off the light when, as an afterthought, he opened the old diary.

Chapter 4

Diary of Suda Mae Jackson

Friday, June 10, 1921

I dreamt last night, me first night aboard this ship, that me mum and I were together once again. In the dream it was years later from yesterday when we said goodbye on the dock in Portsmouth. Years later, yet she had not changed, and she wore the same grey clothes she wore when we waved goodbye as the ship pulled away. I am wondering if me dream will come true. I am wondering if I will ever see me mum again.

Sunday, June 12, 1921

They held no mass for us this morning. Someone said there was mass given on deck for the gentlemen and ladies of the first and second class but we, the ~~emmigrants~~ immigrants in fourth class, are allowed on deck only from noon till one, and six till seven while the gentlemen and ladies dine. The ladies dress very fine and their gentlemen treat them most proper. All the ladies wear beautiful bonnets. I make sure I go below quickly when they start appearing on the deck. Mingling with them is no place for the likes of me. But still I have never missed Sunday communion. I asked around and found the priest's cabin. He seemed quite surprised when I knocked on his door and asked for communion. He was a Polish priest and it was apparent he was quite surprised with a sixteen-year-old English girl bold enough to inquire about mass.

"I don't know that I have ever met an English Catholic," he said.

I informed him cheerfully that there were quite a few of us, especially among those who serve the lords and ladies. He was also surprised when I told him the immigrants aboard ship had been instructed not to mingle with the other passengers. He said he would bring the Holy Eucharist down to us from now on. I then received the Body of our Lord and the priest's blessing.

Our immigrant quarters on ship are near the engines. I know because I can always hear them. Someone said we are well below the water line and if the ship struck an iceberg like the Titanic the sharks would eat us straight away. It is very hot and humid where we stay, but except for that and the lack of privacy (we all sleep in hammocks in one large storage area with only curtains for privacy) it is not a bad place. They call us "emmies" —people who are immigrating. There are only a few English like me. Many are from Germany. There are also Czechs, Norwegians, and some Poles—all were already aboard when the ship docked in Portsmouth. I heard someone say the ship originally departed from Hamburg, Germany, and then made a stop or two in the Viking lands.

There is a Negro family on board. They speak French and are from some colony of France. I never laid me eyes on a Negro person before boarding this ship and methinks many others on board have not either. Many watch them as the Negro family go about their business, staying to themselves. I attempted to speak with one of the children but he ran off to his mother like he was afraid. Methinks they know no English at all, and I speak no French.

Many Irish boarded yesterday when we docked at Cork Harbor. Our quarters were not overcrowded till the horde of wild Irish rushed aboard.

Many people from these other lands have made a great effort to learn some English because of the land that will be their new home. They practice and I help them. I like talking to people from other countries, except for the Irish, of course, who are not a proper people.

As I write there is a storm and the ship tosses about. The hammocks sway madly and many get sick. I miss Mum terribly. Perhaps this is a mistake, this coming to America.

Thursday, June 16, 1921

Food is constantly on everyone's mind, at least with the immigrants. Breakfast is coffee and scones but with no butter or jam. At noon they serve us a broth and coffee. Dinner is usually a boiled fish or salted beef with boiled potatoes. There is nothing wrong with the food but the portions are small and fail to satisfy most. Lines are long. As soon as one meal is over, some get right back in line to wait for the next.

As I stood in the food line for me supper today, a young lad in line several people ahead suddenly sat down on the floor and started crying. The other children near him walked around or over him trying their best to ignore his howling. Finally, as the line brought me nearer the screaming boy, I kneeled down and tried to soothe him. Apparently he was alone. His clothes were ragged and dirty. His floppy peasant cap was a size too large and had worked its way down to cover his eyes and half his face. I took off his hat, which revealed a head with a grand crop of red curls, pale green eyes, and a face covered with freckles. I stood him on his feet but he immediately flopped back down on his backside and screamed the more. Again I stood him upon his feet.

"What is your name, little boy?" I asked.

No answer and once again he tried to flop back but this time I held him strong. All small children had necessary information attached to their clothing and I found this paperwork wired to his ragged coat. The paper said the boy's name was Donald Malcolm McGennis and he was an orphan from some place called Strathbogie in Scotland.

A Scot.

No wonder he was so much trouble.

He was five years old, and his sponsor was someone from Chicago.

"So, your name is Donald Malcolm," I said.

The boy stopped screaming like someone dropped a water gate then he looked at me. He stuck his thumb in his mouth which I immediately pulled out. He stuck it back in and I pulled it out again.

"Don't suck your thumb in public, Donald Malcolm. I'm sure it is acceptable in Scotland but certainly not in America, nor any other civilized country."

Of course, being a Scot, he immediately stuck his thumb back in his mouth. I knew I was wasting me time attempting to teach manners to a

Highlander. I took his other hand and tried placing him back into the line, but he would not release me hand so I had to stand him next to me.

Throughout the day, Donald Malcolm McGennis nary spoke a word, not in English or Scottish.

As I write he sleeps in me hammock.

Friday, June 17, 1921

Donald Malcolm caused quite a row today. Last night I could barely sleep because of the smell (he would sleep nowhere but in me hammock with me), so today I gave him a bath. Or I attempted to I should say. I got his filthy clothes off and threw them in a bucket to soak, then I sat him down in a dry clothes scrubbing pan. All this was done with little problem. But when he saw me bringing a bucket of water the little devil bolted from the pan and ran off stark naked! By the time I sat the bucket down, grabbed a towel and took off after him, he was heading up the stairs toward the deck.

Now I am fast for a girl and I would have caught the little bugger straight away if I was not scared of showing me bloomers as I ran.

Instead of heading to the open deck, Donald Malcolm turned and shot through one of the first-class dining rooms which, as it were, was full of fine ladies and gentlemen. Of course this was a humiliating experience for me as it would be for anyone raised proper, but I had no choice but to chase the naked little heathen through the dining room.

Eventually a very handsome young gentleman came to my aid, reaching out and grabbing Donald Malcolm as the boy raced by his table.

"Thank you, sir," I said winded as I wrapped the towel around Donald Malcolm. Suddenly I thought I owed the fine people an explanation for disturbing their grand midday meal. I turned toward the room in general and explained.

"He's from Scotland."

When I got him below he got the scrubbing of his life, he did! Altho I ended up drenched to the bone meself before I was finished fighting the likes of him.

Saturday, June 18, 1921

Today was glorious. Blue sky and a calm sea. They say we will see New York Wednesday morning if the good weather holds.

I cannot separate myself from Donald Malcolm. He will sleep nowhere but with me. He even follows me into the women's loo (he throws one of his Scottish fits if I try to make him wait outside). The little savage stands there sucking his thumb and tries to watch me do me business, but that's where I put down me foot. I make him turn his back while I untie me bloomers.

And he has yet to speak.

Chapter 5

Diary of Suda Mae Jackson

Wednesday, June 22, 1921

Despite the rules, most of us immigrants were on deck this morning when the New York skyline appeared beyond the bow. We all cheered. I shook all over as we got nearer then passed the Statue of Liberty. The sun was bright and the statue gleamed like there was a light inside.

The ship docked at a place they call Ellis Island. All of us immigrants went ashore. The higher class ladies and gentlemen stayed on board and were taken on to someplace in the harbor to "disembark." Disembark is a new word I learned today. I looked it up in me dictionary. It means "to go ashore out of a ship."

With me bag and Donald Malcolm McGennis in tow, I left the ship and entered a large building that reminded me of a barn, only very clean and white inside. Donald had brought from Scotland only a potato bag for a suitcase. Inside was an old wool blanket and a red handkerchief. Besides the clothes on his back, these were apparently his sole earthly possessions. In this building, nurses checked everyone's skin for diseases. A young Polish girl in the line ahead of me, I would guess her age about ten years old, was hustled away by the nurses. I don't know what they found. She was alone without a mother or father like me and Donald Malcolm.

After the nurses had poked, prodded, felt, and examined us thoroughly, the adults and families were directed one way, and children seventeen years of age and younger who were without parents or adult guardians were pointed another way. To immigrate, all unaccompanied children were required to have an American sponsor who had agreed to take them in. A Swedish girl next to me who spoke English told me her destination was Philadelphia where her sponsors, an aunt and uncle, lived in a grand mansion. A German boy from Nuremberg said he was destined for Milwaukee where a cousin of his mother was a brewmaster at a large brewery.

It was well into the afternoon before me place in the line neared the officials who processed the paperwork that would officially admit me to America. After standing in line for two hours, I noticed Donald Malcolm McGennis squirming.

"Do you need the loo?" I asked. But at that moment he let loose and the front of his trousers grew dark. The little savage spent a penny in his britches!

I rushed him to the ladies's loo — they call the public jerries "restrooms" here in America (a hysterical name for such a place, I can't wait to write Mum and tell her). In the loo I removed Donald's pants and rinsed the stain with water as best I could. I had to put him back into wet pants but at least they were not reeking from piddle.

I lost my place in line but by now most people had been processed. Finally, I stepped up to the counter where a tired looking old man in a blue uniform sat stamping papers. He looked at me as I placed me paperwork on the counter in front of him.

"Name?" he asked as he opened the envelope.

"Suda Mae Jackson, sir." I dipped slightly to show him I was a proper girl. This either pleased or amused him. A slight smile appeared.

"Age?"

"Sixteen, sir."

"Place of origin?"

"Hucknall, in Nottinghamshire, England, sir."

"Parents?"

"Me mum lives in Hucknall, sir. Me da passed two years ago."

"What are your job skills?"

"Me mum taught me to cook, sew a straight stitch, set a formal table, and serve. I can clean and take care of the little ones. Also, I helped the gardener tend some of Lord Willingham's gardens. The gardener said I had a bit of a green thumb. I can work hard, sir. Strong backs run in our family, they do."

"Domestic work." The man said it, stamped something, wrote on a

paper, then took a moment to read. "Your sponsor is a Mrs. Pampe in Evansville, Indiana?"

"Yes, sir."

"Is she a relation—family?"

"She is a second cousin of me father, sir."

"Your reason for coming to the United States?"

"Because of their age, his lord and ladyship, who employed me mum and me after da passed, sold the estate and moved to London to be near a son and his family. Me mum found work at a smaller manor near Hucknall but there was not a position for me. Me father's cousin here in America, Mrs. Pampe, is in poor health and she recently lost her husband. Mum wrote to Mrs. Pampe about sending me to take care of her and the house. Mrs. Pampe's children, who are grown and out of the house, think me coming to help tend their mother is a grand idea."

Suddenly the man looked down and noticed Donald Malcolm who was latched onto me leg with both arms. The man turned his attention back to the papers.

"I saw nothing about a brother. . . ." he said as he flipped through me papers.

"No, sir. This is Donald Malcolm McGennis, an orphan from Scotland. You might say he has attached himself to me."

"I can see that . . . well, you can move on young lady. We'll take care of the little tyke."

"Yes, sir." I tried to pry Donald Malcolm from me leg but he would have none of that and started his caterwauling. "Look, Donald, this nice man will take care of you." This brought only louder howling and a tighter grip on me knee. People all around were watching.

"Perhaps I should watch over him, sir," I said to the man. "Just till his sponsor claims him, that is."

The man nodded so I went about quieting Donald. I handed the man the papers wired to Donald's coat and the man went about his important business with his stamps. When he finished he directed me to another part of the building and I was quite surprised to find it was a large dining area.

The room was nearly full of immigrants from the ship already eating merrily and talking loudly. And what a grand supper it was! Ham and potatoes. Corn and green beans. All a body could eat in a lifetime! Bread with sweet butter. Milk and coffee. Apples for dessert. I fetched a plate for Donald and one for meself and sat us at the end of a long table. The Americans were letting people go back for extra, and as many times as they wanted! We ate till I thought we just might bust open.

When Donald and I finished our dinner we walked up to get our apple. Donald tried to grab two but I scolded him.

"Just one, Donald Malcolm!"

The lady helping serve smiled and said we could have as many apples as we wanted, so I put an extra apple in Donald's potato bag and told him to keep it for later.

We slept that night under clean white sheets on wonderful cots set up in long rows in yet another huge building. I thought I had Donald convinced to sleep in a bed next to mine, but when I awoke during the night he was curled up next to me.

It was our first night in America.

And our last together.

Thursday, June 23, 1921

The train has now been passing through the forest in western Pennsylvania (a state) for quite some time. I checked me map and I think the state of Ohio is not far, but it is hard to tell at night. Outside the window is blackness except for the half moon that appears around this turn or that.

I'm quite anxious to get to Evansville in Indiana (another state). If I make a go of it here in America maybe I can bring over me mum someday. Mum worried that because of its name, Indiana might swarm with the godless savages. All in Hucknall have read the cowboy stories and seen the moving pictures at the nickelodeons. Everyone knows of the American Indians' lechery toward white women. For meself, I would fight to the death before allowing a wild buck to cart me off as his squaw. Before darkness fell, I kept an eye out for their wigwams or tepees along the way but spied nary a one in Pennsylvania.

Just after breakfast early this morning on Ellis Island, Donald Malcolm's sponsor arrived to take him to Chicago. He looked the fine gentleman, this man from Chicago, and his wife a fine lady. Being that Donald was in me charge, the gentleman naturally inquired of me about the boy. I told him Donald would be no trouble at all, even though I knew I would have to go to confession for such a bold lie. The gentleman told me they had no children and they had found Donald through some grand international adoption agency. The lady was overjoyed when she saw Donald and she knelt to embrace him. I knew the little Scot would try to bolt so I was prepared when, sure enough, he tried to run. I harnessed him quick and knelt down beside him.

"Donald Malcolm McGennis!" I say to him. "You have to go with these fine folks." He tried to pull away and run again but I held him strong. "Look at me, Donald Malcolm." He finally looked me in the face. "This fine gentleman and lady will love you and take care of you and make something of you," I tell him. "You'll be civilized and proper instead of an unruly Scottish lout."

Suddenly a sad look came into Donald Malcolm's eyes—a look I had yet to see from him. It was a look of sorrow and resignation, it was. Like he was accustomed to having to go with people he did not know. Suddenly the fight was out of him.

I picked up Donald Malcolm and handed him to the gentleman.

For all me days on earth, I won't forget the look in the eyes of Donald Malcolm McGennis, who had nary spoken a word in the time I'd known him.

Chapter 6

Late in the fourth quarter Joe Rocker received a signal from Coach Baker on the sideline. Baker served as co-defensive coordinator with Coach McConnell. McConnell sat high up in the pressbox for an eagle's view of the goings-on below. With Baker on the sideline, the two coaches communicated through their headsets.

Joe stepped into the huddle and called the defense.

"Thirteen, cover four! Ready, break!"

The eleven players in silver helmets clapped in unison and broke the huddle. Reitz held a precarious five point lead against a tough Central High team. The Bears had a balanced offensive, having shown in their first two games that they could run and pass with equal effectiveness. Now, with a third down and four yards to go for a first down, it was tough to guess.

Would they run or pass?

Joe had been watching number 84, the Central tight end, and had noticed the Central player's actions at the line of scrimmage changed depending on if the play was a run or a pass. On running plays, as soon as 84 broke the huddle, he jogged quickly to the line and spent little time getting into his stance. But if the play was a pass, Rocker noticed the tight end would jog to the line more slowly, all the while looking down field to see where the Reitz safeties were lining up. Joe had spotted this tendency in the film sessions earlier in the week, and so far in this game the Central player held true to form.

Central broke their huddle, and 84 was the last guy down in his stance.

Joe knew Central was going to pass.

The Bears' quarterback took the snap and spun to hand off the ball to the tailback who was following the fullback off tackle. This action would normally require Joe Rocker to charge the line of scrimmage and "train wreck" the fullback, who was the tailback's lead blocker. Joe ignored the backfield keys and dropped back to play the pass. It was a gamble and if he were wrong, Central would get their first down, and Joe would get a major chewing out from the coaches.

The Central quarterback stuck the football in the tailback's stomach, then withdrew it. It was a fake. The play would be a pass as Joe had guessed.

Joe had his eyes on the tight end who was attempting to "drag" across the middle of the field. Normally, the run fake would have drawn the linebackers toward the line and out of the way of a pass to the shallow middle of the field. That's what the Central quarterback was expecting to happen, so he didn't see Joe until it was too late. Joe stepped in front of 84 and caught the ball as if it were intentionally thrown to him. Joe headed for the endzone sixty yards away. There was a great deal of traffic to weave through and a Central player managed to slow him down by grabbing a handful of Joe's jersey.

Joe spotted Pete Younger, one of the Reitz safeties, racing up from behind and lateraled the football to him. Younger raced the remaining forty yards for the score.

It was the last score of the game. The Reitz Panthers were now 3-0 and Pete Younger, because of Joe Rocker's gamble and heads-up lateral, was interviewed by a newspaper reporter after the game. Younger had to pay for Joe's first double cheeseburger at Steak-n-Shake later that night.

Chapter 7

Diary of Suda Mae Jackson

Saturday, June 25, 1921

Just finished a letter to Mum. I miss her something terrible.

I am now in Evansville, a grand place on a river the likes of which you've never seen. Compared to this Ohio River the Thames is but a stream. In town, cable cars are everywhere . . . and Ford automobiles. Seems everyone has a Ford auto, altho I did see a horse drawing an ice wagon just like back home in Hucknall. Saw nary an Indian on the trip from New York and none in Evansville so far.

I met Mrs. Pampe this morning. Me mum always told me, "Suda Mae, you never get a second chance to make a first impression." So I hope I left a good first impression with Mrs. Pampe as she is a most proper lady one can tell straight away. She talked very kindly to me despite discomfort from her feet—apparently a long time affliction. She has strong facial features, as one would expect of someone with a German heritage (on her father's side).

Mrs. Pampe's house is on Wabash Avenue. The house is very large, its furnishings of simple good taste. Me duties will be to clean and sew mostly. I will cook occasionally. Mrs. Pampe says much of the cooking is done by ladies from her church. The lawn is trimmed by a neighbor boy. I asked Mrs. Pampe if I might be allowed to plant some flowers as the lawn is in dire need of them, especially in the side yards. She seemed pleased by the request.

To my surprise there is a dog—a three-year-old beagle named Cleo. Cleo is the last of a litter sired by Mrs. Pampe's late husband's favorite rabbit dog. I'm sure Mrs. Pampe keeps the critter because it reminds her of happy days. I will be responsible for the dog's care. I told Mrs. Pampe I have never undertaken such a task—caring for animals that is—but she did not seem overly concerned.

The house has five bedrooms, four of which were empty when I arrived. I was given a room on the same floor as Mrs. Pampe's bedroom but at the opposite end of the hall. Mrs. Pampe says the room was her youngest daughter's, who is now married and living in Missouri. I knew straight away Missouri is a state and not a city because of the Tom Sawyer book I read at school back home.

Me room is wonderful and very cozy indeed. The bed has a canopy. The room has a sitting chair and a desk with a reading lamp where I now sit and write. In front of me is a window that spies out to the rear yard.

I think America is everything they say it is and I feel there is every reason for a body to be happy here. But I miss Mum.

Saturday, July 2, 1921

Have been twelve days in America, one week of that in Evansville. Mrs. Pampe seems impressed with me. Yesterday I finished alterations on a dress she says she hasn't worn in years. It took me the better part of two days. She says I could be a professional seamstress, and a fine one at that. She has been very kind and frets that I am working too hard.

Everything has been quite calm till today. I went out early to plant some flowers before the heat of the day (which is considerable here). As I knelt at a garden in a side yard I hear the most outrageous racket you can imagine. A boy, looking to be about my age, was banging and kicking on the gate to Mrs. Pampe's yard. I stood and approached the intruder and of course I immediately took him to task.

"And what, may I ask, do you think you're doing?" I asked sternly. At first he stared at me with a quizzical look, then he had the gall to look me up and down like I was there for his inspection. He smiled like he approved of what he saw. This caused me to be both embarrassed and angry and I could feel me face flush. Redder than a strawberry I imagine I was. I let him know of his rudeness.

"I say, you impertinent young man, what business do you have here? Why are you banging on Mrs. Pampe's gate?"

"You talk funny."

I felt another flush.

"Leave immediately or I'll have Mrs. Pampe summon the constable."

"The what?" He seemed to take great amusement in my speech. I turned and started toward the house.

"Hey, wait a minute," he called after me. "I'm here to cut the old lady's grass. I do it every week or so. Been doing it since I was twelve." He gave the gate another kick and it finally opened. "This gate sticks. You have to kick it to get it open."

"Mrs. Pampe is not to be referred to as 'the old lady,' you rude young man."

"Sorry, I meant no disrespect. I like the old, uh . . . Mrs. Pampe," he said as he ran to catch up to me. "My name is Tommy O'Donnell. Who are you?"

An Irishman! That certainly explained everything. Never had God put a more uncivilized people on His earth, surpassing even the Scots for rudeness and ignorance. Donald Malcolm McGennis was the way he was because the Scots were too crude to teach their young differently. Taken out of Scotland, a Scot could, with proper upbringing, at least hide his true nature, but everyone knew that the Irish could never hide their crude character. They were beyond the reach of propriety.

Of course I did not answer his question. I turned away and quickly went into the house to find Mrs. Pampe who was reading the morning newspaper.

"Ma'am, there is a rude young man outside who claims he shaves your lawn."

"That has to be the O'Donnell boy. Yes, he has cut my grass for several summers, my dear. Is there a problem?"

"He is Irish, ma'am."

"Oh . . . yes, I guess he would be with a name like O'Donnell."

"Ma'am, we must be concerned about thievery. Stealing runs in his blood—him being Irish, that is."

Mrs. Pampe, the poor dear, seemed less than alarmed and even amused at me warning, but perhaps this is to be expected from Americans who are apparently unfamiliar with the character of such people as the Irish. She told me that the O'Donnells have lived in Evansville for two generations, and that Tommy was the eldest of three sons who had lost their father a few years back. Since then Tommy had man-of-the-house responsibilities and worked odd jobs around the neighbourhood to help support his family.

Despite this news, I determined then that it would fall on me to keep an eye on this Tommy O'Donnell for Mrs. Pampe's sake. Even an Irishman who worked, which was rare, and did not speak with the coarse Irish brogue could not be trusted. I was also determined that no Irish boy be thinking he got the best of an English girl. I returned to me work in the garden.

Tommy O'Donnell was pushing around a reeler he had brought out from a storage shed in Mrs. Pampe's rear yard. He now had his shirt full off as I suppose is common among his ilk, not caring that he was exposing himself to a proper girl. He attempted a conversation each time he pushed the cutter within shouting distance of me, which I ignored of course. This did not deter him in the least and he chattered away until I finished me work and went into the house.

Lord, what are we to do with the Irish?

Chapter 8

Diary of Suda Mae Jackson

Sunday, July 3, 1921

I walked to church this morning with Mrs. Pampe. Even though her parish church is but a skip away, a man with a Ford auto usually delivers her because the poor dear struggles with her feet so. But this morning she felt chipper about walking with her cane so we donned our Sunday best. Mrs. Pampe seldom leaves her house save for church and had not wore a bonnet since her husband passed, instead wearing a simple lace scarf to church. But early Sunday morning I picked flowers from one of the gardens and decorated Mrs. Pampe's bonnet. I thought she would be pleased, but when I showed her the bonnet she cried. She said her husband loved to see her in her bonnet. Now I knew the reason the dear woman stopped wearing it. She had worn her bonnet for her husband. I felt bad for making Mrs. Pampe cry and I told her I would get rid of the bonnets (I had decorated mine also). Mrs. Pampe said no, she would wear her bonnet and I would wear mine.

When it came time to leave for church, Mrs. Pampe came down the stairs looking quite lovely in a beautiful dress. And she was wearing her bonnet.

Saint Boniface is a grand place indeed with twin spires as high as Heaven. Inside, the colors are bright behind the altar. The stained glass sparkles. The pews shine and sport beautiful ornate carvings. The Altar Society ladies had done a brilliant job with the flowers. Mrs. Pampe told me the Germans built Saint Boniface and was rightly proud that her father was among them. The Germans are a hardy and industrious lot.

We arrived twenty minutes early to allow time to say the Rosary. The church slowly filled as I knelt with me beads. Mrs. Pampe cannot kneel but says her prayers from the pews. I had just finished me prayers and sat back in the pew when a commotion caught my attention. I turned and saw

Tommy O'Donnell entering with two unruly little urchins who had to be the brothers Mrs. Pampe told me about. Tommy O'Donnell smiled when he saw me. I turned up me nose and turned back around to prove I was not pleased to see him. And wouldn't you have it, Tommy O'Donnell made his way over and squeezed himself and his two brothers into the pew directly behind us. One of the little Indians immediately proceeded to drop the kneeler heavily on the floor causing another loud noise. People turned to look our direction.

"Good morning, Mrs. Pampe, lovely bonnet, ma'am," I heard Tommy O'Donnell say behind me. Just like the Irish. Instead of being on his knees praying he was making conversation like it was the race track he was at. Mrs. Pampe turned and greeted him in return and thanked him for the compliment.

"The credit belongs to Suda Mae here," Mrs. Pampe said, referring to our hats. "She decorated my bonnet, along with her own."

"They are very nice, Miss Suda Mae."

I could feel his eyes on the back of me neck. I'm sure he was waiting for me to turn around, but of course I ignored him. I knew if I turned I'd probably catch him staring at me bosoms, and right in church too, the Irish lout. Sweet Madonna pray for us!

Despite the constant fidgeting of the two small brothers of Tommy O'Donnell, the service was quite nice. Luckily when we left the church Tommy O'Donnell's direction home was opposite to ours so Mrs. Pampe and I enjoyed a peaceful walk. We spent the rest of the day in pleasant conversation. Mrs. Pampe told me many stories of her dear late husband, her children, and other members of her family.

Tuesday, July 5, 1921

Yesterday was quite bizarre. Last night the locals celebrated the Colonies breaking away from the Crown and the revelry included some outlandish behaviour. The Americans are most fond of their firearms and take great delight in letting them off in their rear yards. They point them to the sky like they are shooting at the angels in Heaven. They fire away, not to bag a fowl for a supper stew, but simply to relish the noise made by booming shotguns and rifles. These startling noises seem to fill the Americans with great delight. Mrs. Pampe tells me this practice of shooting off such weapons is common on July 4—their Independence Day holiday. Even very young boys are allowed to act as triggermen.

Earlier yesterday, in the afternoon it was, a large group of men dressed in white robes and hoods gathered up and down the street in front of Mrs. Pampe's house. I found out they gathered on Wabash Avenue in preparation for a march down Franklin Street. It was a strange sight indeed, this horde of men in their odd costumes. I asked Mrs. Pampe about these men. She tells me their club is the Coo Clucks Clan and I'm wondering if they are the local chicken farmers but Mrs. Pampe tells me no, they are a political group that opposes bootleggers and Catholics. She says they are general troublemakers who wear their masks so they can traipse around secretly while they cause their mischief. Mrs. Pampe says with us being Catholic it is best to avoid these fellows. I asked Mrs. Pampe why the constables do not cast these people into the hoosegow. She tells me this club of men has considerable influence with the police since many policemen and local authorities are members of this coo club.

Friday, July 8, 1921

Today was me day to visit the grocer on Franklin Street. Mrs. Pampe gave me a list and money (I've learned the American money now), and off I went. I pulled along Mrs. Pampe's grocery wagon.

I handed me list to the grocer and while he filled a box I walked outside to pick out me chicken. A young boy was in charge of the chicken pins and, after I looked the birds over and pointed, the boy bound the feet together amid much squawking and complaining on the chicken's part.

The bird was for chicken and dumplings, an American dinner Mrs. Pampe said she would teach me how to cook, so it was me job to prepare the bird as soon as I returned to the house. With bird and axe in hand I went to the backyard. On a tree stump just for that purpose I held the bird down and was just about to swing me ax when the bird turned its head, pecked me hard on me left hand, and bolted. The grocery boy had done a poor job of tying the chicken's feet. The strings came loose and now the chicken ran free throughout the backyard.

Now I am fast for a girl, and I've run down chickens, geese, and turkeys before (geese are the easiest to catch) so I took off after the bird. I would have caught the creature straight away if it were not for the wet grass and a few muddy pools left behind by last night's hard rain. I just about had the bird when suddenly I lost me feet and fell head first into a mud puddle. As soon as I raised me face out of the mud I heard him. I wiped the mud from me eyes and turned me head to see Tommy O'Donnell standing at the alley gate, watching me and laughing like a madman.

Covered in mud from head to toe, I calmly walked over to the stump and picked up me axe. "I'm going to cut your ears off, you Irish criminal."

With axe in hand, I chased Tommy O'Donnell down the alley for two blocks till he was too far ahead and I had to give up.

Chapter 9

Joe Rocker turned a corner and headed toward the attendance office. It was seventh period and Joe spent the time working as an aid to Ms. Ackerman. He was returning from his rounds to pick up attendance cards from various classrooms. His hands were full of cards and he was not paying attention as he opened the attendance office door.

Joe was forced to quickly step out of the way as a girl tumbled out of the doorway. Because her hands were full, the girl had been pushing the door open with her back when Joe jerked open the door. As she fell, she dropped her books and papers scattered everywhere.

Students standing nearby burst out laughing. Joe didn't recognize the girl. She had pink hair, black lipstick, orange eye shadow, and a nose ring. He laid the attendance cards down on a nearby desk and attempted to help the girl pick up her papers and books.

"Sorry," Joe said as he knelt down to help her. "I didn't see you leaning against the door."

She shot him an angry look and snatched her book out of his hand.

"I can pick up my own books, you muscle-headed bozo. I don't need your help!"

She quickly collected her things and, after giving Joe one last look of disapproval, walked away.

The girl falling out of the doorway was the only highlight in an otherwise routine day at school. At football practice, Joe jammed his finger on an offensive lineman's helmet, causing the finger to balloon, but ice was applied and nothing seemed to be broken. The trainer taped a couple of fingers together and Joe returned to practice.

Joe had planned on bringing Suda's diary to school to show Mr. Holden, his history teacher, but Suda's story had captivated him.

He would read more that night.

Chapter 10

Diary Of Suda Jackson

Saturday, August 27, 1921

Today cooled a bit, altho the heat still seems to press down on a body. By the Saints I never imagined this type of heat and I miss the cool summer breezes of home. Mrs. Pampe tells me the Evansville autumns are quite nice and the weather should start cooling in two or three weeks. I look forward to that for sure, for sure.

Except for the heat, the summer has been pleasant enough. I spend me time taking care of me household chores altho Mrs. Pampe gives me plenty of time to meself. At least three or four times a week I take Cleo for a stroll around the neighborhood.

One day, as Cleo and I passed a small house several blocks from Mrs. Pampe's house, I noticed a little boy of six or seven years, no more, sitting at a window. The house was in disrepair and in dire need of paint. The fence gate was broken and fallen away, but the lawn was freshly cut and well cared for as to almost seem out of place with the house itself.

"Is that your dog?" the little boy asked from his window.

"It is indeed. Well, actually she belongs to Mrs. Pampe, but I'm in charge of her, I am. Would you like to come out and pet her?" With that the little boy disappeared from the window. I waited, thinking to meself he was coming out to pet the dog but I saw no more of him. After several minutes I went on me way.

Two days later, upon my next walk with Cleo, the little boy was again looking out his open window. Once again he asked if the dog belonged to me. I assured him again that Cleo was in my charge and once more invited him to pet her. Again he disappeared from view but did not emerge from the house. This went on every time I passed the house. The little boy would appear in the window, ask me if the dog was mine or: "What kind of dog is that?" or "What's your dog's name?" The little boy never left the house and

I never spied anyone else about the house or yard.

One evening at supper I inquired about the little boy with Mrs. Pampe, but she knew nothing of the house or the circumstances of any people who lived there.

Then it was, that today, as I made me walk with Cleo, I spied none other than Tommy O'Donnell reeling the grass in the yard of the little boy's house. The little boy was in his window watching Tommy O'Donnell and when I came into view, the little boy yelled out with great excitement: "Tommy, that's Cleo the dog and the girl that talks funny!"

Tommy O'Donnell stopped pushing his reeler and turned me way. He grinned wide when he saw me like he had some type of right to consider me a friend and equal. Irish men tend to ignore accepted social mores between members of the opposite sex, even those who have not been properly introduced, because they know nothing of genteel and proper ways.

"Hello, Miss Suda Mae Jackson." Then with a phony Irish brogue, "Top o' the mornin' to ya."

I would have ignored him as usual, but the phony accent raised me dander. Was he trying to make fun of me British speech by faking an offensive Irish brogue? I looked at him sternly.

"Are you making fun of me, young Tommy O'Donnell?"

"No, no," he said and started to laugh. "I like the way you talk. My family is originally from Ireland and my grandfather used to greet us each day with "top o' the mornin'."

"I know very well what you are, Tommy O'Donnell. I would not be bragging on the fact that I was Irish if I were you. And I'll accept none of your ill manners, or your conversation while you stand there with no shirt on."

"So if I put my shirt on you'll talk to me?"

"I certainly will not!" I put me nose in the air and turned to walk away with Cleo.

"Can Henry pet the dog? He tells me about it every time I'm over here. I didn't know it was you, but I should have figured it out when he told me

about the girl who talks funny."

There was that grin again. And making fun of me speech for sure this time! I felt me blood boil.

"I'll have you know, Thomas O'Donnell, that the likes of you does little to change the poor notions proper people have of the Irish. And what's more, I have asked that little bugger several times if he wanted to pet this animal. He ignores me and rudely disappears from the window. He must be Irish like you! Probably a blood relation from County Galway or some such ungodly place on the western shore."

That should put Tommy O'Donnell in his place! But instead of acknowledging that I had the upper hand, at first he had the gall to look at me like he didn't know what I was talking about. Then a slight smile appeared on his face, but this time it wasn't the cocky Irish grin. There was a bit of sadness about him.

"Wait here," he says. "I'll get Henry."

He walked to the porch, put on his shirt, then into the house he went and walked out carrying the little boy. Even with trousers covering Henry's legs I could tell the thin and limp limbs were useless. Henry was a cripple, and I felt lower than a snake's belly for what I had said about him. Tommy would tell me later it was polio that had robbed Henry of the use of his legs.

Tommy O'Donnell knelt down on one knee beside Cleo and sat Henry on his other knee. The little boy hesitated at first, but Tommy assured him the dog was friendly by patting Cleo's head and scratching behind her ear. Henry eventually reached out and Cleo licked his hand frantically, causing the boy to laugh with delight.

My glib tongue had forsaken me and I stood in silence as Henry petted the dog. It wasn't long before a lady appeared walking up the street. She looked tired and worn. It was Henry's mother it was. She was arriving home from her work, having walked four miles because she could not afford the trolley. A tired smile appeared on her face when she spied Henry happily playing with me dog. She greeted Tommy O'Donnell and thanked him immensely for shaving her lawn.

"Mrs. Niemeier, this is Miss Jackson."

"Please call me Suda, ma'am," I says. "Pleased to meet you I am." I curtsied.

Mrs. Niemeier went on to sing the praises of Tommy O'Donnell. She tells me she is a widow and that she and Henry have a hard go of it, her not having a widow's pension and all. She tells me how Tommy O'Donnell takes care of her lawn without charge and fetches groceries for her when she can't make it to the market. And how he plays with Henry or sometimes brings his two little brothers along to play with her son. She says she admires Tommy, who is also without a father, for being like a big brother to Henry.

I looked at Tommy O'Donnell and he looked away as if embarrassed.

Leave it to the Irish to mix things up.

I received another letter from Mum. She writes that all is well except she misses me so. I cried when I read her letter, and I cried for Henry Niemeier.

Chapter 11

Diary of Suda Mae Jackson

Monday, September 12, 1921

And what a day it was. School opened today and what a school it is! There must be 200 students with many more to come, I hear, when the farms finish their harvest in a few weeks. The school is called West High School altho it is officially Francis Joseph Reitz High School. And as one would expect of a school named after a German, it is a clean and orderly place. The building is new for all intents, having been raised just three years ago according to the cornerstone. West High sits like a castle on a hill high over the town with a brilliant view of the river and beyond to the land of Kentucky (which they say is not a state but in fact a commonwealth—I don't know the difference yet but I will find out in me studies I am sure of that). Our school colors are purple and gold, and our mascot name is the Westsiders.

Got me books: a reader, a book of arithmetic, and me science book. Even the books are free in America altho everyone is expected to supply five cents for their two pencils and paper. I think five cents a bit much for two pencils and a stack of paper; one can buy three pencils for a penny at the apothecary on Franklin Street, but since the books are free I guess they have to make up some of the money now and again.

Mrs. Pampe gave me the five cent American coin to pay for me pencils and paper. The coin is called a nickel and it presents the face of an Indian on one side. This surprised me I must say. I thought Americans hated their Indians. From the American cowboy stories I know the Indians are a murdering horde of savages, therefore me surprise at seeing the face of one cast on an American coin. These Americans are a strange lot.

I found me classrooms with little trouble and met the schoolmasters who are plentiful—must be a dozen or me name's not Suda Mae.

The boys may wear common trousers but white shirts are required.

As for the girls, the hems of our dresses or skirts can be no higher than six inches above the ankle and socks must be worn so that no skin shows. Our blouses must be long-sleeved and buttoned tight to the neck for modesty. All this is very warm as to be uncomfortable this time of year, but dress rules are understandable. We must not give the boys reason to neglect their studies. All the girls bring their bonnets but we are not allowed to wear them during class. When we enter the classroom we store our hats on a rack for that purpose near the back of the room.

And lo and behold who would walk into me science class but the Irish Tommy O'Donnell. Lucky the girls and boys are separated on opposing sides of the room or the big oaf would try placing himself next to me I'm sure of that—and probably embarrass me with his grinning the entire time too! After class he waited in the hallway till I came out the door and he asked if he could carry me book.

"I'll not be needing any Irishman to carry any book for me, Mr. Tommy O'Donnell," I says, but I knew he would persist so I had no choice but to let him carry me book to me next class.

Except for Tommy O'Donnell pestering me, I was treated well enough by the instructors and the other students. Several students were very curious about me "accent." This happens often in America and it always strikes me as strange. I never thought of meself having an accent. In fact, it is the Americans who have the funny accent if I'm to be asked.

As we walked to me next classroom, Tommy tells me he plays football. I am a great fan of Hucknall's football team and I have in fact played the sport meself I told Tommy O'Donnell. A curious look, somewhat of amazement, came over his face.

"You played football?" he asked with an amused sound to his voice. One which I did not appreciate.

"I'll have you know, Mr. O'Donnell, that for two years I was the goalie for the Hucknall girls' junior team, I was!"

"Goalie?" Tommy O'Donnell laughed. "There's no position in football

called 'goalie.'"

I did not appreciate being laughed at by an Irishman and I let him know this straight away.

"Thomas O'Donnell, you know as much about football as you do proper manners. I'll not be speaking to the likes of you again, and I'll thank you to hand over me book." With that I snatched me book from him, turned up me nose, and left him where he stood.

Chapter 12

After his third corndog, Tim Grainger was now looking for the food booth that sold tamales. Joe Rocker chomped on a barbecued turkey leg, and Antwain Davis, a sophomore on the football team, made short work of a huge Texas tenderloin sandwich.

"Give me a drink of that cider, Davis," Grainger said. "I'm choking to death."

Antwain handed over his jug of apple cider. "Just don't backwash it," Antwain told Grainger.

The three friends wove their way through the mass of humanity on Franklin Street. It was the first week of October, which meant the annual Westside Nut Club Fall Festival was in full swing. The Festival raises thousands of dollars each year for local schools and charities and is a major event for the city of Evansville, having grown over the years until it was now purported to be the second largest street festival in the country—second only to Mardi Gras. Food booths and carnival rides stretched for several city blocks, shutting down Franklin Street to auto traffic for the week.

They continued down the street, stopping several times to talk to friends from school. Finally, they reached the area of the larger rides and bought tickets for the Zipper, the emptier of any full stomach. When the ride came to a stop, Tim Grainger staggered off and deposited his lunch on the street directly in front of a pair of teenage girls. The horror on the girls' faces was obvious. Joe and Antwain were laughing so hard they were bent over gasping for breath.

"Don't move," Grainger told the girls. "I'm not finished yet." He vomited again. The girls screamed and scurried away disgusted.

Chapter 13

Diary of Suda Jackson

Sunday, September 18, 1921

As Mrs. Pampe and I pulled up to church this morning—today we rode with Mr. Muensterman and his wife in their Ford auto because Mrs. Pampe, the poor dear, did not feel up to the walk—we noticed the priest in front of the church surrounded by a large group of parishioners. We could see many people pointing and some shaking their heads. A few women cried.

Of course we were quite concerned. After Mr. Muensterman parked his auto and we reached the front steps, I saw what was causing the dismay. Someone had painted, in bright red paint no less, a message on the beautiful, heavy oak doors of our church.

Mackerel Snappers are UnAmerican
Join an American Church or go live with your poap

Below the words a crude picture of a cross with what looked like flames was drawn along with the letters KKK. Me first thoughts were that besides misspelling "pope" the coward was obviously a complete twit leaving behind his initials. I later found out, however, that the three K's stood for the name of the same club that had gathered for the march in front of Mrs. Pampe's house on the American holiday in July. Back then I had wrongly spelled the name of the club with C's in my diary. The club is in fact spelled K U K L U X K L A N. Of course "mackerel snappers" is an insulting label for Catholics and one I had heard used many times by the Anglicans at home in Hucknall. It refers to our practice of eating fish on Fridays and Holy Days.

I was not about to join in with the women who stood crying and wringing their hands. Instead I felt me blood boil and I found meself standing with the men who spoke of revenge against this KKK. What I wouldn't give to find the scoundrel who desecrated the church, me being a girl none the matter. I would thoroughly enjoy horsewhipping the cur to within an inch of his life.

Jesus forgive me.

Eventually all entered the church. During the homily, Father Hillenbrand mentioned the defiled doorway and reminded us to "turn the other cheek" and "return good to those who abuse you." I'd return something alright, and it'd do me heart good too, altho I don't know how much good it'd do for the blackguard who painted the doorway.

Sweet Mary pray for me.

As I set and stewed I realized that the befouled door wasn't the only thing that made church not ordinary on this day.

It was the first Sunday since I had been in Evansville that Tommy O'Donnell was not at mass.

I was not aware of exactly where Tommy O'Donnell lived so I inquired of Mrs. Pampe. I hitched Cleo to her leash and set out about me way. Spying the dog being walked about would keep the big Irish oaf from wrongly presuming I was worried about him, because I certainly was not!

As I neared the address Mrs. Pampe directed me to, I noticed many of the neighbor people in their yards or on their porches looking toward the O'Donnell house. A few neighbors were inside the O'Donnell's gate talking to Tommy and a woman who I assumed rightly to be Tommy's mother. Then I saw the reason for the commotion.

Painted on the front wall of the O'Donnell house was a message disapproving of Catholics and the three K letters. It was all very similar to the one found that morning on the church door and I suspect the same villains were involved. Also, a small statue of the Virgin that I learned later had sat for years in a flower garden in the O'Donnell's front yard lay in pieces—smashed on the brick walk.

Tommy was consoling his mother who was quite upset as you would imagine. He spied me approaching and walked over to the fence.

"Do you know who did this?" I asked.

"The Klan."

"Yes, but do you have any idea of the persons themselves?"

"No, I called the police. They came by and said they would look into it but I don't expect to hear much from them. Some say about a third of the police force are members of the Klan and another third are sympathizers."

I told Tommy about the message on the church door.

"I wish I could lay my hands on the cowards," Tommy said. I could see the anger in his green eyes. At that moment I had no doubt that the K men would find themselves in a painful way if ever they came upon the Irish fists of Tommy O'Donnell. Everyone knows brawling comes natural to the Irish and you could never really whip an Irishman. Even if you got the best of an Irishman in a fray they were too dumb to know they were beat and would keep getting up and coming back at you no matter how bloodied their faces be.

Tommy asked me to come in the gate and he introduced me to his mother. She was quite polite despite her distress. Tommy O'Donnell's mother did not rain down evil Celtic curses on the heads of the criminals as one would expect of an Irish woman at such a moment.

I asked Mrs. O'Donnell if me help was needed but she said nothing could be done just then. Tommy was gathering the pieces of the statue and she said they could not acquire any paint for the house until the next day when the Heldt and Voelker opened. The Heldt and Voelker is the hardware and farmer's store on Franklin Street. I have been there to buy twine and stakes for Mrs. Pampe's rosebushes.

As I walked away I sinfully hoped that Irish Tommy O'Donnell's wish for revenge against the K men be granted.

Monday, September 19, 1921

Mrs. Pampe showed me her newspaper this morning. It reported several "random acts of vandalism and mischief" committed around town the day before. Two Catholic churches besides Saint Boniface suffered vandalism as did the homes of over a dozen people—mostly Catholic widows who had no husband to appear on the porch with a shotgun if a trespasser was heard skulking about outside a window in the night. Mrs. Pampe made a comment that we were probably lucky the trouble had passed us by, her being a widow and all.

This immediately took me mind to Henry Niemeier and his mother who were also Catholic so I walked by his house on me way to school. The Niemeier house had not been bothered thank Heaven. Henry was in the window as always and asked me where was Cleo. I was glad to see the house showed no signs of disruption. I told Henry I was on me way to school but I would bring Cleo by later.

School buzzed with talk of the weekend's mischief. The O'Donnell house was not the only among the students of West High to suffer at the hands of this despicable K clan. Talk was that at least three other students and their families awoke Sunday morning to discover devilment done to their property. Edna Schultz, a girl in me arithmetic class, complained that the ~~clan~~ Klan hurled red paint onto her father's new Ford auto as it sat parked on the street in front of their house.

None of the people who have endured wrong at the hands of these K men seem optimistic that justice will be served because of the present high station these men are apparently granted by the local authorities.

It is not right that they are allowed to get away with these things.

Not in America.

Chapter 14

Diary of Suda Mae Jackson

Wednesday, September 21, 1921

Tommy O'Donnell has been very quiet in school since the Klan men visited his house in the dark of night. This week he has spoken little to his lads at school and he has not been hounding me to carry me books—that is "my" books I must remember, says Miss Unfried, ~~me~~ my English teacher. I enjoy English class and I'm learning all about colons and semi-colons. Miss Unfried says if we use colons, semi-colons and dashes when we write we'll impress our reader with our intelligence as long as we use them correctly.

I have struck up a friendship with Hazel Ewig, a girl who sits by me in history class. Hazel fancies a young man who is a member of the school football team and she asked me to go with her to watch the team practice after school. She tells me she would feel awkward by herself so I agreed to be her company. After school we walked down a hill to where twenty or so young men ran about in the oddest costumes I had ever laid my eyes on. Certainly none of the footballers in Hucknall wear such garb. Most of the boys wore a strange leather cap the likes of which one sees worn by the aeroplane barnstormers. The uniform shirts were stuffed like pillows around the shoulders. Baggy pants ended just below the knee.

And my goodness! Whatever it was they were doing it certainly was not football! They hold the ball in their hands and try to run with it, which any dolt knows is against the rules in football. If that were not queer enough, as soon as the boy with the ball begins to run, the lunacy then begins in earnest. It seems the other boys delight in chasing the boy with the ball so they can toss him to the ground and jump on him. Sometimes so many boys pile on the boy with the ball that even the ball itself has been smashed till it is no longer round but shaped like a peanut. I could not believe my eyes at the goings on. I looked at Hazel who expressed no surprise whatsoever at the madness.

"What is this Hazel? I thought the boys were to play football."

Hazel looked at me oddly. "This is football, Suda." Then Hazel pointed discreetly to the boy of her fancy. "Look, there's Fred. Isn't he handsome?" I kept my comments to myself. Hazel's Fred had a bloody nose, a black eye, and looked the worse for wear.

In the midst of it all was the Irish Tommy O'Donnell. He was easy to spot because he wore no cap like the others.[1] *I could not avoid thinking that this was a game perfectly suited to the Irish and indeed Tommy O'Donnell seemed to be one of the ringleaders. He carried the lopsided ball on several occasions and seemed quite content to charge headlong into the fray, and when an Irishman gets tossed to the ground they lack the good sense to stay down. Tommy O'Donnell jumped up off the ground each time. Likewise, when Tommy chased after another boy who carried the ball, Tommy dove with great spirit into the boy's legs to smite him to the ground.*

Hazel and I stayed till the end of the madness, for Hazel was of a mind to talk to her Fred. As they walked, I hung back so as to mind my own business.

"Hello, Suda." I turned to find the Irish Tommy O'Donnell approaching, still dirty and somewhat skinned up from the muddle that the Americans claim is football.

"Hello yourself, Tommy O'Donnell. After ignoring me for two days it is now that you decide to talk to me, looking like a pig that has been mucking about in the slop."

He seemed surprised. "I thought you didn't want me to talk to you, Suda."

"That has never stopped you before, has it now?"

Tommy smiled. We walked in silence a short distance toward the place where the rest of the footballers headed to clean themselves and change out of their strange costumes. I sensed that Tommy O'Donnell had

---

1 In football, wearing a helmet was optional in the 1920s.

something to say and was having a hard time saying it.

"What is it you want to ask me, Tommy O'Donnell?" I might as well help him get it out. First Donald Malcolm McGennis on the ship and now Tommy O'Donnell. Since leaving Hucknall, it seems my lot in life is to help the crazy Scots and the wild Irish.

"What do you mean?"

Of course I knew what it was he wanted. "You're of a mind to court me but don't have the courage to say it."

Tommy's face turned red. "Uh. . . ."

"Where is it you want me to go with you?" I sighed to show him my impatience. "I guess I'll have no choice but to go. You'll pester me to my death until I agree to it anyway."

"Well . . . there is a football game here Saturday afternoon. I'm the team captain. I thought if you wanted to come watch us play, maybe we could go out for a milkshake afterwards."

"And what time is it you would deliver me home, Tommy O'Donnell?"

"Games are normally over between three and three-thirty. You would be home by supper."

"And who are our chaperones?"

"We normally go to the soda fountain at Meyer's Drug Store after a game. There will be adults and several of the guys from the team with their girls."

"Is that what I am now, Tommy O'Donnell? Your girl?"

"No, no, of course not. I'm just saying there will be people there."

"I'll have you know, Tommy O'Donnell that I'm a proper English girl and would never allow myself to be courted by an Irishman. But I will attend your game as a neighbor. Like I said, I guess I have no choice, and at least at the game we'll be apart and you'll have something to keep your mind busy. You'll not be able to leer at me and think the evil thoughts like you've been doing for the past five minutes."

"Suda Mae! I . . . I have not!" Tommy stopped walking and now his face was twice as red.

"Don't lie, Tommy O'Donnell, altho it is in your Irish nature."

"Suda, I was not leering at you, or thinking. . . ."

"Be careful young man. I'll hear none of that from your vulgar Irish tongue. As for your milkshake, I will consider it and let you know later in the week. I must be assured we are accompanied by proper people. These 'football' players, if that is what Americans insist on calling that madness, do not fill me with much confidence in their mental tightness. Now, if yourself is finally finished leering at me, I'll be on me way." I slipped again; it is "my."

I turned up my nose and walked off, leaving the Irish Tommy O'Donnell where he stood.

Chapter 15

Diary of Suda Mae Jackson

Saturday, September 24, 1921

There had been talk on Friday of a Saturday rain, but when I walked to the school stadium just after fixing Mrs. Pampe's lunch, there was nary a cloud and the day quite pleasant. I was glad of it for sure as I did not want my bonnet ruined, nor did I have a desire to spend the afternoon watching Tommy O'Donnell and his football lads wallow in the mud like razorbacks.

The concrete stadium seems to be carved right from the hill itself and is very big indeed, sitting just below the school, which towers over the field like a grand castle. Hazel Ewig spied me and called my name. She sat in an area that seemed occupied mostly by students. She waved frantically for me to join her.

"Isn't this exciting, Suda?" Hazel almost could not control her glee. On the field there were only the boys from the other team. That team was from a place called Mount Vernon. I saw none of our boys so I looked around for what Hazel thought so exciting.

"What happens now, Hazel? Where are our boys?"

"They get dressed in the cafeteria then come down these steps to the field," Hazel pointed. The steps were concrete as were our seats.

Hazel had just said it when our team appeared at the top of the steps and ~~begin~~ began their walk down. Students lined both sides of the steps to cheer the boys as they made their way to the field. They looked quite chipper in their uniforms, their football shirts being a dark purple with bright gold numbers. Tommy O'Donnell was number seven and in the front of the pack, leading the team down it seemed. I suppose it be his captain's job. Hazel spied her Fred and yelled and waved till she drew his attention. He winked at her as he passed and I thought the silly girl would swoon. Tommy O'Donnell best not wink at me.

At the start of the game the Mount Vernon boys lined up and kicked the ball at our boys. Tommy O'Donnell caught the ball after one bounce and ran back toward the Mount Vernon boys who chased after Tommy till they finally caught him and knocked him to the ground. Down near the field some girls wore sweaters and skirts in the school colors. They held large megaphones and led the people shouting for the team. Hazel told me the girls are called "yell leaders."

After awhile I could tell that the main point of the sport was to catch the boy with the ball and jump on him after he was knocked to the ground. This took place regardless of which team was using the ball at the time. The purpose of jumping on the boy with the ball is still unclear to me but the boys on the field and even the people watching from the seats took great delight when someone was thrown down and jumped on. Apparently, by the end of the game, our boys had jumped on the Mount Vernon boys more times because Hazel pointed to a man down by the field holding up big cards that said our school won 47 to 6.

When the bizarre spectacle ended, Hazel and myself joined other students near the field to wait for the football boys to clean up and change clothes. Tommy and Fred joined us and we began our walk to Franklin Street and Meyer's Drug Store.

"What did you think of the game, Suda?" Tommy asked.

"Very civilized."

Tommy laughed.

Meyer's Drug was already crowded with students, but we found a booth and the four of us ordered our milkshakes. Tommy and Fred were quite lively, as was the rest of the crowd, because of winning the football match. Fred had a tooth knocked loose during the match but he said it had happened before and would tighten back. Some iodine colored a cut over Tommy's right eye.

We talked for some time. Tommy and Fred made Hazel and myself laugh many times with their silliness. The afternoon was quite enjoyable but finally it was time to leave.

"I'll walk you home," Tommy said.

Mrs. Pampe's house on Wabash Avenue is but a short walk from Meyer's Drug Store. We talked little and about half way home Tommy O'Donnell reached over and took my hand. My first thought was what my mum would think of me letting an Irishman hold my hand.

"Maybe sometime we can go dancing," Tommy said.

I was shocked and pulled my hand from his. "And where exactly would we go to do that?" I demanded to know. Dancing between teenagers was strictly forbidden at all school and church functions.

"There's a dance hall over in Shawnee Town, Illinois, that admits teenagers."

"So you would take me to this Shawnee Town and make me your floozy."

"No! Of course not."

"Say no more, Thomas, if it's a tart you're looking for, you still have your looking ahead of you."

"Suda, you always twist my words."

"It just makes you nervous because I know what you are really thinking, young man."

Tommy shook his head and remained silent. I guess he considered it the safest thing to do. He walked me to the door and I thanked him for the afternoon.

"This was a nice day and I thank you Tommy O'Donnell, but don't be thinking you'll be kissing me now. Proper girls never kiss on a first date."

"Of course not, Suda Mae. The thought never entered my mind."

"Don't be telling another lie, young man. You know you want to kiss me." I turned and walked into the house, leaving the green-eyed Irishman where he stood.

Chapter 16

Diary of Suda Mae Jackson

Wednesday, November 9, 1921

Yesterday was a black day, it was. My walk to school takes me past the house of Henry Niemeier, and as I neared Henry's home I spied a constable's auto parked in front of the house. As I drew closer I saw why the constable had been summoned. Several of the front windows of Henry's home were missing, smashed to bits with pieces of the glass lying both inside and outside the home. A red cross was clumsily painted on the wall near the front door. I ran to the door and found it open. I peered through the screen but did not see Mrs. Niemeier or little Henry, just the constable who was looking about.

"Sir, my name is Suda Mae Jackson. I am a friend of the Niemeiers. Would you be kind enough to tell me where Mrs. Niemeier and her son Henry might be?"

The constable spied me for a long moment before telling me the boy had been taken to the hospital. "He received some cuts from the glass. His mother is with him."

I flew from the porch and ran for all I was worth to Tommy O'Donnell's house. Now like I've said, I'm fast for a girl but my satchel of books slowed me considerable. When I got to the O'Donnell house Tommy had already left for school. I told Tommy's mum what had happened at the Niemeier's and asked for directions to the hospital. Mrs. O'Donnell said it was too far to walk so from her purse she gave me a token for the trolley and instructions on where to catch it.

When I arrived at the hospital I asked about Henry and was shown into a room where a nurse was about the business of wrapping his wounds. He had bandages on both legs, both arms, and one tight around his forehead. His mother sat teary-eyed next to him. When Henry spied me he smiled and asked about Cleo. His mother looked up then rose and took my arm to walk me outside the room, out of Henry's earshot.

"He'll be fine, Suda. He has quite a few cuts but most are minor. Only one needed stitches, the one on his forehead. He got that cut when broken glass from his bedroom window fell into his bed and he rolled over to let himself down to the floor. He got the rest of the cuts sliding across the floor on broken glass trying to get to me to see if I was hurt. Can you imagine? The little dear was worried about me." Mrs. Niemeier cried bitterly.

I stayed with Mrs. Niemeier and Henry till he was released; then I rode the trolley home with them. The word of the ill deed had spread and people from Saint Boniface were already at the house boarding up the broken windows. The kindly parishioners promised that new glass would be installed soon.

After going home to retrieve a nickel from my coin purse, a nickel I needed for another trolley token, I made my way to 1 Edgar Street. The newspaper had often published this address as the headquarters of these Ku Klux Klan people. Indeed, when I arrived at the address, numerous KKK signs and posters decorated the entrance of the house. I raised a rock and flung it through the largest window producing a loud crash and removing over half the glass from its frame. It took only a second for three angry-looking hooligans to burst through the doorway. They looked to be in their late teens or early twenties. I fired two more rocks. The first missed but the second made a pleasing (to my ear at least) thud when it hit the nose of one of the rogues. He yelled out in pain and blood spurted from his face like someone poked a hole in a vampire.

"She broke my nose!" he bellowed.

I yelled some very improper words at the lot of them. Words that should never come from the mouth of a proper young lady. Sweet Jesus forgive me.

The other two ran toward me and I looked around for something to arm myself when a man appeared from the doorway.

"Stop!" the man said to the two roughnecks who, when they reached me, grabbed me roughly like they intended to haul me into the building. I

fought for all I was worth and said more bad words. One of them had me by the sleeve of my dress and as I fought the sleeve ripped away from the shoulder.

"I said STOP!" the man at the entrance repeated. He was dressed in a very fine suit of clothes. He looked more like a reverend or a solicitor than someone associated with this KKK riff raff. Neighbors were starting to appear on nearby porches to watch the commotion, something the finely dressed man had taken note of.

"Mr. Stephenson," one of the hooligans turned and said, "she broke the window and hit Hubert there in the face with a rock." Hubert knelt and held his nose. The man they called Mr. Stephenson pulled a handkerchief from a coat pocket and handed it to the bleeding rascal.

"Let her go, now!" the finely dressed man ordered and walked toward us. The scoundrels released me and stepped back.

"Quite a way to introduce yourself, young lady," the man said and smiled. "We do have a bell at the door. Next time you come calling you might consider using it."

"I'll do worse next time if the KKK curs ever bother Henry Niemeier and his mother again."

"Henry Niemeier? I'm not familiar with the name. I'm sure nobody in this organization is responsible for whatever befell this person."

"The windows to his house were smashed and little Henry was cut badly from the broken glass. A cross was painted on their house. A cross that looks just like that one." I pointed to one of the posters. The man did not turn to look at it.

"I'm afraid, young lady, that this is a problem we have to deal with from time to time. Vandals who have nothing to do with our organization find in us a way to divert attention away from themselves." The man handed me a card. No other information was on it besides a name: D.C. Stephenson. "Your accent . . . you're obviously from England."

"England?" said one of the young hooligans. "I know who she is. My cousin goes to the new high school and he told me that some gal from England goes to school there. I bet it's her. I can find out where she lives!"

The man shot the youth a grim, withering look. The youth shut up immediately.

"I'm sorry about your friend, but again I assure you we had nothing to do with it. Please send me the bill for your dress."

"I am quite capable of fixing me dress meself, I'll have you know." They had made me so mad I had forgotten my proper American grammar. With that I directed my attention to the rascal who threatened to find out where I lived; I kicked him between the legs a good one and he crumpled to the sidewalk. Then I turned and walked away, leaving them where they stood.

It was now my great desire to find Tommy O'Donnell. I was in no mood to discuss my absence with the principal, so I waited for Tommy in a small woods at the bottom of the high school hill. I knew Tommy passed through there on his way home. I waited for two hours. It was late, after football practice, before he finally appeared. He had heard nothing about the events of the day. I told him everything: about poor dear Henry and my encounter with the Klan men on Edgar Street. Tommy hugged me but said I shouldn't have confronted the men at their headquarters.

"That was foolish, Suda. You don't want to mess around with those people. You could have been seriously hurt."

We stopped by the Niemeier's home to check on Henry who was sleeping in his mother's bed. We talked to Mrs. Niemeier but I could tell Tommy was beside himself with anger—anger which he did not want to burden the poor woman with so the talk was a brief one. He walked me home.

"What are you going to do, Tommy O'Donnell?" I asked him on Mrs. Pampe's porch. He did not answer. "You listen to your own advice, Tommy, and don't rush off and do something foolish."

"I'll see you tomorrow, Suda."

With that he walked away and left me where I stood.

If that would have been the end of yesterday's black adventures it well would have been aplenty. But last night Mrs. Pampe and I awoke to shouts of neighbors and their pounding on our doors and windows. Looking out my window I saw Mrs. Pampe's storage shed, the one by the alley, engulfed in flames. The shed served as a storage place for Mrs. Pampe's garden tools and the place where Cleo slept! I raced down the hall to make sure Mrs. Pampe was getting up. She was putting on her robe.

"Call the fire wagon, Mrs. Pampe! I'll check on Cleo," I says. I raced down the stairs in my nightgown and out the back way I went. Neighbors were throwing buckets of water on the flames with little effect. It was decided the shed was beyond saving and efforts should go toward keeping the fire from spreading to the house or neighboring houses. I called for Cleo and heard a weak bark from inside the shed!

"Mrs. Pampe's dog is inside the shed!" I yelled at the men with buckets. One man told me that it was too dangerous to try and save the dog. I ran past a man with a bucket. He tried to stop me but I reached the door of the shed. The door too was afire. The shed door was normally left ajar so Cleo could go in or out during the night but someone had purposely fixed the latch and trapped her inside. When I took hold of the metal latch it burned my fingers but I managed to get the door open. I had to step back to avoid the smoke bellowing out of the doorway. I called out again to Cleo but heard nothing. Another man grabbed my arm but I pulled away and entered the shed. I was forced to hold my breath because of the smoke and I thought I would faint from the heat. Lucky for me Cleo was lying near the door where the poor thing had tried to escape. She was limp, overcome by the smoke, and did not respond to my calling her name. As I knelt to pick her up a hot ember from above fell on the fringe of my nightgown and lit it afire. I toted Cleo out as fast as I could with the hem of my gown burning. A man with a bucket threw the water on me and put out the flames as other men in their fire wagon pulled up in the alley.

I knelt down with Cleo a safe distance from the fire. She looked up at me with the big eyes of a beagle, struggled for one last breath, then died in my arms.

I sat there for several long minutes then wept the tears of a broken heart: why, Lord, do the innocent like Henry Niemeier, a little crippled boy, have to suffer? And this small creature I held in my arms, who did nothing in life but bring joy to humans, why are they subject to such cruelty? I want an answer, Lord! Forgive me.

When I finally looked up, Tommy O'Donnell stood next to me. He had seen the glow of the fire from his house and had come running. As he stood looking down at me he did not look like the boy who a few days ago had held my hand as he walked me home.

Even in the bright glow of the fire, there was now a darkness to Tommy O'Donnell that frightened me.

Chapter 17

As was usual on mornings before school, the "Link" at Reitz High was crowded and busy with chatter. The Link was a glass-enclosed walkway that joined the original building built in 1918 to the new addition finished in 1994. This was the morning gathering place for students waiting for that day's classes to begin. Somewhere along the line an unwritten social rule had developed concerning the Link's marble benches. Each seemed to be claimed by a small group of students who sat at the same bench every day. It was the height of rudeness to claim someone else's bench as your own. Freshmen especially took great pains to avoid this social faux pas.

Joe Rocker sat on one of the marble benches along with Rick Turner, Tim Grainger, and Zach Stratton.

"Hey, Zach," Tim asked, "are you still working at Schnucks?" Zach Stratton had worked at the grocery store as a bagger over the summer.

"No, man," Zach answered. "Can't work during football season. No time. You know that."

"Well, I meant will you have a job there when the season ends."

"I should have. They knew when I hired on I couldn't work during football season and I left on good terms. They'll probably take me back. I think I only called in sick once all summer, that day we all went jet skiing on the river."

Tim Grainger interrupted. "Yeah, he was real sick that day." The others laughed.

It was Rick Turner's turn: "Yeah, the rest of us don't have it so good as our boy Rocker. Our dads don't own their own business. Mr. Easy Street here [pointing to Joe] can go, or not go, to work anytime he wants."

"You guys wouldn't last a day doing plumbing," Joe spoke up. "The first time you had to lug a four-hundred-pound cast iron bathtub up three flights of stairs, or better yet, the first time you were on your belly in a dark crawlspace and you shined your flashlight on Mr. Rat who was smiling back at you, you'd be high-tailing it home to the couch and your Playstations."

"Rats suck," stated Zach. The others nodded their agreement.

"But since you brought up the subject of working for my dad," Joe told his friends, "we bought and are remodeling one of those big old houses on Wabash Avenue. You know, the ones over by Saint Boniface. Anyway, I was tearing out a wall a few weeks ago and found an old diary. It was written by a girl in 1921 who was a Reitz student."

"What?" exclaimed Tim. "I didn't know this place was so ancient."

"Reitz was built in 1918," Joe confirmed.

"So what's in the diary?" Rick interjected. "Any old money?"

"No, but the story is interesting."

Joe's three friends looked at each other then at Joe as if he was telling a joke and they awaited the punch line.

"No, I mean it," Joe repeated. "It tells about her coming to Evansville from England and going to school here on the Hill. Stuff like that. She also had a run in with the Ku Klux Klan."

"She was black?" Zach asked.

"No, black people couldn't even go to school here back then, or to any school with white kids. We learned that in middle school, dummy. She was Catholic and she wrote in her diary about the Klan hassling the Catholics back then."

"Why did they do that?" asked Rick. "I thought the Klan was against black people and the Jews."

"I don't know that much about it," Joe admitted. "I have Mr. Holden for Indiana Studies. Maybe I'll talk to him."

"Sounds like a good idea," said Rick. "Now, can we talk about something really important? Like who's going to loan me fifty cents so I can get a Coke after Strength and Conditioning class?"

"Hey, Joe, good to see you!"

The greeting came from Mr. Holden, a Reitz social studies teacher and local historian. Mr. Holden was well known for his knowledge of Evansville and Vanderburgh County history. The town's newspaper dialed Mr. Holden's number for those hard-to-find facts on obscure events of long ago. Even libraries and local historical societies were known to call on Mr. Holden when an answer to a question on regional history could not be found elsewhere. Mr. Holden extended his hand. Joe shook it.

"It's not seventh period, what brings you to this neck of the woods?" Mr. Holden asked.

"I had some questions about the Ku Klux Klan," said Joe, "and I figured you would know the answers."

"Well, thanks for your confidence in me. I hope I don't disappoint you. What are your questions?"

Joe had dropped by Mr. Holden's room on the spur of the moment. Now he wished he was better prepared. "Uh . . . the Klan back in 1921, apparently it was a pretty large organization in Evansville?" He was shooting from the hip, knowing nothing about the Klan except what he had read in Suda's diary.

"Yes," Mr. Holden began. "And not just in Evansville. The Klan pretty much ran the show across the entire state in the early twenties. They wielded a lot of political influence. The Klan was responsible for getting a man named Males elected Evansville mayor in 1925, and they also succeeded in getting their candidate elected governor of Indiana that same year. Here in Evansville the Klan actually held police powers. Klansmen went around arresting people."

"You're kidding." Joe was flabbergasted.

"Hard to believe, huh?"

"How did they get away with all that? Was everyone afraid of them?"

"Yes, many were hesitant to oppose the Klan back then, for various reasons. Today, the KKK has no power. No one goes out on a limb by opposing the Klan. Back in the twenties that wasn't the case. But they had their opponents. Many Roman Catholics around here banded together to stand up to the Klan."

"I guess black and Jewish people did too," Joe added.

"Not really," said Mr. Holden. "Remember, Joe, the 1920s was a long time before the Civil Rights Movement. The local Klan didn't bother African Americans much back then because they felt black people 'knew their place' so to speak here in Evansville. I guess the Klan felt it didn't have to waste much of its mischief on them. There were only a few scattered incidents of the Klan focusing on African Americans back then, at least in this area. And as far as Jewish people, there just wasn't a large enough community of them here in Evansville in the twenties to count in the mix of things. No, back in the twenties, the Klan focused most of its fury on Catholics and bootleggers."

"Why did they hate Catholics?"

"The main plank of the Klan's political platform back then was patriotism. They liked to think of themselves as the guardians of the flag, mom, and apple pie—defenders of the American Way. They felt Catholics were not 100% American because, the Klan thought, if it ever came down to it, Catholics would give their ultimate allegiance to Rome."

"Amazing." It was all Joe could think of to say.

"Yes it was. Especially since, just a few years prior to all this, so many young Catholic boys volunteered for service and went over and fought in World War I. Many sacrificed their lives, just like Protestant and Jewish boys."

So far everything fit with Suda's diary. The Klan and the Catholics did battle.

"Anything else?" Mr. Holden asked.

"Uh . . . I guess not. Thanks, Mr. Holden."

"No problem. Mr. Hammonds has some materials in the school library you might want to check out. Also, the Red Bank Library has a good supply of books on the Indiana KKK of the 1920s. And, of course, you can find a great deal of information on the Internet. I might suggest looking up the guy that was a real driving force of the Klan, first here in Evansville then later the entire state."

"Okay, what was his name?" Joe dug in his backpack for a pencil.

"D.C. Stephenson, the Grand Dragon."

Chapter 18

Diary of Suda Mae Jackson

Thursday, November 10, 1921

Besides a large bit of soot that stained the bricks on the back of Mrs. Pampe's house, the fire destroyed no buildings besides the shed. I've scrubbed and scrubbed the bricks and the black stain is coming off, but slowly.

Early yesterday morning I buried Cleo under the apple tree in Mrs. Pampe's side yard. It broke my heart to see Mrs. Pampe cry as I threw dirt on poor Cleo. The gentle dog was a link to her dear late husband.

I will not tell Henry Niemeier about Cleo's fate. At least I'll put off the hateful moment as long as I can. I could not stand to see Henry cry as I know he would. Eventho I will owe a penance for lying, I have already thought up a story and will tell Henry that Cleo is visiting her beagle family in the country. Methinks Henry will believe it. The child is too innocent to know a lie when he hears it.

I hoped all day yesterday that Tommy O'Donnell would come around, but Mrs. Pampe and I saw nary a sight of him. It wasn't till much later, well into the evening, when Mrs. Pampe and I received the phone call from Henry Niemeier's mother. She sounded quite anxious. When we found out why, Mrs. Pampe almost swooned and I felt like I would retch.

Tommy O'Donnell and his mother and brothers are missing.

Saturday, November 12, 1921

I went to school yesterday but had a time of it concentrating on my studies. I cannot get Tommy and his family out of my mind. Where are they? What has happened to them?

This afternoon Mrs. Pampe sent me on an errand to the grocery on Franklin Street. Up and down that street a large crowd was gathered and people traipsed back and forth in costumes. It was a strange sight, indeed. The people were quite gay, but with all the troubles of late I did not share the merriment.

I spied Hazel, who was with her Fred, and asked her what the gathering was about. Hazel told me it was a new festival of sort started just this year. I did not quite understand Fred who said something about the festival being started by a west side club of men who are nuts.

I certainly won't argue with him about that.

Sunday, November 13, 1921

Tommy and his family are still missing. Mrs. Pampe and Mrs. Niemeier are both beside themselves, the poor dears, as one would expect. When the authorities came by to talk to Mrs. Pampe (who called and reported the family missing) they assured Mrs. Pampe that they would find the O'Donnells, but anyone could tell they found the situation most unusual. The constable told Mrs. Pampe that it was not that unusual for a young man of Tommy's age to disappear. The constable told us that sometimes young men run away to join the carnivals and circuses, or to ride the hobo rails for adventure. But for an entire family to disappear in the middle of the night seemed to fluster them to no end.

I go by the O'Donnell house every day. I guess I'm hoping to find Tommy and his family at home around the supper table like nothing has happened. I also go by the Niemeier's house each day to check on little Henry and his mum. Henry wanted to know were Tommy was. I told the angel that Tommy would return home soon and would come first thing to visit.

Then he asked if Cleo was home from visiting her family. I cannot bring myself to tell Henry about Cleo.

Monday, November 14, 1921

It was in the newspaper today.

A fellow in the Ku Klux Klan is missing and the circumstances surrounding his disappearance are mysterious indeed. Blood was found on the front porch of the house where the man lives. Apparently the man was shanghaied from his home on Read Street in the middle of the night. The newspaper tells of a ~~neighbour~~ neighbor hearing an argument. The missing man's name is Hubert Jenkins and his photograph was alongside the story.

He is the man whose nose I broke with the rock.

D.C. Stephenson is quoted in the newspaper as claiming the Catholics are to blame for the disappearance of Hubert Jenkins. Stephenson told the newspaper that Hubert Jenkins had been "attacked" by Catholics in the past and that there is a Catholic conspiracy against "hardworking, red-blooded Americans" like Hubert Jenkins.

Bloody lies if ever any were told.

Wednesday, November 16, 1921

The constables came by today to speak with Mrs. Pampe. Mrs. Pampe and I were both glad to see them stop their Ford auto in front of the house and we met them on the porch. But instead of giving us news about the O'Donnells, they showed Mrs. Pampe a picture of Hubert Jenkins, the missing Klan man. They wanted to know if Mrs. Pampe had ever seen this Jenkins fellow or knew of any ill feelings between Tommy and the man. Mrs. Pampe assured them she knew nothing of this Jenkins and she was sure Tommy had no ongoing spats with anyone, and especially not people of this sort.

The constable holding the photograph looked at me and asked who I was. I told the man I was a relation of Mrs. Pampe. He asked me if I knew Tommy. I almost lied and said no, but I would have shocked Mrs. Pampe who would have wanted to know why I told such a lie. When I admitted I knew Tommy, the man showed me the picture of Jenkins and asked me if I had ever seen the man or heard Tommy speak of him. I told the constable I had never seen or heard of the missing Hubert Jenkins. Mrs. Pampe knew nothing about my run in with Jenkins that day on Edgar Street so I was safe with this lie. Sweet Mother Mary pray for me.

Then he told Mrs. Pampe that a witness had seen Tommy fighting with Hubert Jenkins on the day both he and Jenkins disappeared.

Tommy O'Donnell was being charged with kidnapping and murder.

Friday, November 18, 1921

There was a picture and home address of Tommy and the same of Hubert Jenkins in today's newspaper. The authorities must have gotten Tommy's picture from school as it was his football picture. The story told of witnesses seeing Tommy attack Hubert Jenkins at his home, of Jenkins disappearance, and of more witnesses seeing Tommy O'Donnell dumping a large object, that looked to be a body, into the Ohio River near the shanties just down river from Pigeon Creek.

Sunday, November 27, 1921

It has now been just over a fortnight since Tommy O'Donnell and his family vanished. Of course all the talk at school is of Tommy and the murder. I find myself always distracted at school and it is hard to keep my mind on my studies. Just this Wednesday past, Mrs. Kempe, my arithmetic teacher, cracked my desk with her yard stick and warned me about my daydreaming. She said a paddling might get my attention. I should have been more embarrassed, but I really didn't care.

I am not the only one at school who misses Tommy. The football team is doing poorly without its captain. I'm not sure why I went to the game last Thursday since I knew the absence of Tommy would hang over the day. Perhaps I was hoping he would appear in his football costume and run out on the field.

Silly.

The game was horrible for our side. With everyone worried about Tommy, including our football boys who seemed full of gloom without their captain to give them a cheerio, the football boys from Central beat our boys 104 to 0. Our boys could not stop the Central boys and especially a Central boy named Herman Byers. But I must say that the Byers boy was a gentleman. Fred told Hazel and me that the Byers boy came over to our sideline after the game to console our boys, telling them that West High could have a fine football team someday.

The game was on Thanksgiving Day, my first Thanksgiving, and it was a sad day indeed. I am told this American holiday is always a happy affair but with the troubles all around it was hard for most who know the O'Donnells to offer a merry face.

It becomes harder each day to visit the Niemeiers. Henry's bandages are now gone, but his mother tells me Henry misses Tommy and Cleo and he is not eating as he should. I can see the poor color of the little boy's face.

The authorities have been back several times to ask Mrs. Pampe questions, and sometimes when I pass by the O'Donnell house I see them parked down the street, watching the house as if they hope to capture Tommy when he returns home.

And I'm wondering if I'll ever see Tommy O'Donnell again.

Chapter 19

Diary of Suda Mae Jackson

Monday, November 28, 1921

Sleep has not been easy since Tommy O'Donnell and his family disappeared. Last night was no different.

It was just after midnight and the blackest part of the night when I heard it. I was in my bed but my eyes were wide open. It was faint but I heard it clear.

It was a knock on my window.

The knock put a fright to me but still I flew from my bed and reached the window straight away. I could see only a shadow on the roof outside the glass but I knew who it was as I raised the window.

"Tommy!" I probably said it much too loudly. He had climbed the rose trellis to the first floor roof and made his way up the steep tiles to my second floor window.

"Not so loud, Suda. Don't wake Mrs. Pampe. No one must know I'm here."

"Come in." I opened the window all the way.

"No," he said. "I just wanted to tell you . . ."

I never let him finish. "Thomas O'Donnell, you get yourself off that roof." I grabbed his shirt with both hands and pulled him into my room through the window. Not wanting to make a ruckus and wake Mrs. Pampe, he did not fight me. I closed the window then realized I was in my nightgown.

"Turn around," I ordered as I fetched my robe.

"Suda, I shouldn't be in your room. What if we are caught?"

"You're going nowhere, young man, until I get some answers." Tommy sat on the floor just under the window. I sat on the floor beside him. "What happened, Tommy? Where have you been? Where is your family?"

"It's a long story, and I'm not even sure about some of it."

"We have the time. What did you do, Tommy O'Donnell?" Tommy looked at me without expression.

"After everything that has happened this fall—the vandalism at church and my house, then the attack on the Niemeier's house and Henry getting hurt, and the fire here and Cleo and all—I couldn't take anymore. After I left here the night of the fire, I went to the Klan house on Edgar Street."

"The same place I went?"

"Yes. Anyway, I don't know what I had planned. I guess I didn't really have a plan. For a minute I thought about just knocking on the door and punching the first guy to answer the door. But I noticed the lights at the back of the house and men in the back yard standing around talking. So instead of going to the front door, I went around to the alley that runs behind the place and sneaked up to where I could hear what was being said. The alley was dark and they couldn't see me."

"You're a foolish one you are, Thomas O'Donnell."

"What about you, Suda? You did the same thing."

"I did not. I was there during the day and out in front where people were about."

"Yeah, right. Like you thought about all of that beforehand."

"And how do you know I didn't, young man?"

Tommy managed a weary smile.

"So I'm hiding in the alley," Tommy continued, "when I hear these guys talking and laughing about how they were going to run the Catholics out of town, or at least put them in their place like the Negroes. There were four of them in the backyard. Then a couple of them started bragging about locking a dog in a shed then setting the shed on fire. (I felt sickness in my stomach when Tommy said it.) They seemed very proud of themselves. When I heard that I couldn't take anymore, Suda, so I ran into the yard and went after the two guys who bragged about killing Cleo."

"Thomas O'Donnell! You could have been killed! I wouldn't put it past those mongrels to do away with somebody!"

"I think I scared them at first," Tommy said, ignoring my alarm. "I ran at them yelling like a wild Indian. One guy ran into the house. I tackled

one of them and started pounding his face. The other two guys just stood there watching for a moment, like they were frozen and didn't know what to do. Then the other two found their senses and rushed me. I found myself fighting the two of them. The guy I pummeled was in no shape to fight any more. I was so crazy mad that I held my own even when the guy that had run in the house came back out to join in the fight." Tommy stopped telling his story and leaned his head back on the wall.

"So what happened then, Tommy?"

"The noise started waking the neighbors. Lights came on in houses nearby. One of the guys I was fighting started pulling the others away. He said something about a 'Mr. Stephenson' being mad if there was trouble there at the headquarters. I don't know who this 'Mr. Stephenson' is but these guys seemed worried about him being unhappy so they pulled away and started toward the house."

"I know this Mr. Stephenson," I said. "I have seen his name in the newspapers and he is the fancy man I had the bad luck to meet when those scoundrels tore my dress. The newspapers calls him the 'Grand Dragon.'"

Tommy seemed to be thinking for a moment about what I just told him before he spoke again.

"I have to admit it was probably lucky for me the fight was over. I was spent and I think I would have been in a bad way if it had gone on much longer. They headed into the house but not before threatening to find out where I live and burn my house down with me and my family in it."

"Tommy!"

"That night I had my mom pack up my brothers and go to my aunt's house in Illinois. That's my mom's sister. My aunt and her husband live in a big farm house outside Carbondale. It's about a hundred miles from here. No one will find them there and you must not tell anyone, Suda, not even Mrs. Pampe. Promise me."

"I promise. Tommy, what is all this about kidnapping and murder?"

Tommy expression changed to one of sadness and anger.

"It's all lies, Suda. They are accusing me of kidnapping Hubert Jenkins

from his house on Read Street. I have never been to Jenkins' house. Jenkins is the one I tackled and punched when I first ran into the backyard at the Klan house on Edgar Street. I socked him a few good ones but that's all. He had gotten to his feet by the time the fight was over and was cursing at me as I ran away."

"So how can they accuse you of kidnapping and murder? Where is this Jenkins fellow?"

"I don't know, Suda. All I know is at first I was just hiding from the Klan. Now I'm hiding from the Klan AND the police."

Tommy closed his eyes as if he were resting, then after a moment he opened them and looked at me.

"Do you believe me, Suda?"

"Of course I do, Tommy O'Donnell. We must find out what has happened to this Jenkins fellow."

Tommy looked startled and grabbed my arm. "What do you mean 'we'? You're not going to get involved in any of this, Suda Mae, do you hear me?"

I did not answer as I was already trying to think of what to do next.

"Suda," Tommy said sternly, "promise me you will not get involved in any of this. Promise!"

"I do not promise anything of the sort, Thomas O'Donnell. What type of wife would I make if I failed to help my future husband?"

Tommy's jaw dropped slightly. "What did you say?"

"Oh, come now, Thomas. You know you love me, and when an Irishman gets a thought in his head there is no changing his mind. I knew that day at Henry Niemeier's house when you carried him out to pet Cleo that I would have no choice but to marry you someday—whether I want to or not."

Tommy stared at me for a long moment, his mouth still open, before he returned to the original subject.

"Promise me, Suda, you will not get involved in any of this. If you don't promise me I'll go right now and turn myself in to the police."

"You can't do that!"

"Then promise me."

"Alright then, I promise." I had no intention of keeping my word. After I die I know I'll spend eons in Purgatory for all the lies I tell.

Tommy seemed content with my answer and for a moment again closed his eyes as if resting.

"How long has it been since you slept, Tommy?"

"I don't know," he said. I could see the weariness in his face. He got up to leave.

"Where are you going?"

"My uncle loaned me his Ford. I parked it behind the church and walked here through the alleys so no one would see me. I'll drive back to Carbondale until I come up with a plan."

"How far is this Carbondale did you say?"

"A hundred miles."

"You'll certainly not go back there now. Look at you. You're asleep on your feet. You'll get some sleep first. You can sleep in my bed. I'll use the rocker. I'll wake you just before dawn so you can be on your way before first light."

"Suda, I can't stay here. What if Mrs. Pampe would find us? She might send you back to England to avoid a scandal."

"I'm not letting you take out and fall asleep behind a steering wheel and get your hardheaded Irish skull bashed open in some auto crash."

"You're the one who is hardheaded."

"Watch your tongue you Irish lout. You're speaking to a loyal subject of King George."

I think Tommy wanted to smile but he was too tired. He was also too tired to argue anymore. He spent the night in my room, sleeping like a dead man, while I sat in my rocking chair. I did not sleep but spent my time thinking about the troubles and what I could do to remedy them.

It was five o'clock when I awoke Tommy O'Donnell. It took quite a shaking to rouse him from his deep sleep. Through the same window he entered he left just before first light. Before he went out onto the roof, he held my hands and gave me my first kiss.

◊ ◊ ◊

There the diary abruptly ended. The remaining pages—and it was easy to tell there once had been more—had been torn from the spine of the book.

What happened to the missing pages, and why were they missing? What happened to Tommy and Suda?

Joe Rocker had a mystery on his hands. A mystery he had to solve.

Chapter 20

It was six o'clock. Football practice had ended.

A wind blew and promised rain but so far had not kept its promise. It was late in a gray day—gray the color of November in southern Indiana. But this day was a lighter gray and not cold. The temperature was in the upper fifties. It was windbreaker weather.

With the windows rolled down and the stereo blasting, Joe Rocker drove south on First Avenue. When he passed Franklin Street, he spotted Willard Library, turned left, then parked the pickup in the library's parking lot. When Joe was a sophomore, his English teacher assigned the class some genealogy research at Willard Library. Joe learned that Willard was the place to search for the paper trails of birth, marriage, and death records of people from Evansville and Vanderburgh County. Joe figured if it worked for uncovering facts concerning the Rocker family it might also work for information about Suda and Tommy.

The library sat in a small park—its gnarled trees surrounding the building. Multi-colored leaves fled from their limbs, set asail by the stout breeze. Branches groaned and creaked. Only two other cars were in the small parking lot when Joe pulled in. Joe knew of the legend of the Grey Lady, the phantasm that supposedly haunted the library.

If this place isn't haunted it should be, Joe thought. Though the architecture gave the impression that the building was designed for the Addam's Family, the facade, mostly brick, was well kept. There was no peeling paint or rusted ironwork.

Leaves crunched under his feet as Joe walked through the parking lot. Thirteen concrete steps led up to a set of tall, heavy wooden double doors set in an arched vestibule. A wide staircase led to the second floor. To the right, another staircase accessed the basement, and to Joe's left the entrance opened to a room on the main floor. Joe chose this room and entered a large and surprisingly grandiose area. The ceiling was extraordinarily high. Like Atlas holding up the world, massive posts throughout the room carried the second floor on their shoulders. Walls and trim were white with gold accents. Several windows around the room ran from floor to ceiling. The wood floor creaked (of course). Four brass chandeliers gave the room the ambience of a 19th century ballroom despite the musty smell of an old library. It was the sharp, inviting smell of wood and ancient paper not offered, sadly, by the newer concrete and carpeted libraries.

The checkout counter and various sized tables sat at the near end of the room. An elderly priest sat at the end of one long table intently reading a book. Joe saw no one else, including no one behind the checkout counter. He had no idea where to begin his search for information on Suda and Tommy so he wandered about.

On one wall hung four large portraits. Inscriptions on the frames identified the portraits as those of Willard Carpenter, his wife, a daughter, and son-in-law.

"That's not the Grey Lady."

The voice from behind startled Joe and he whipped around. A plump, older woman with a rosy countenance and a mischievous twinkle in her eye stood behind him. *How did she sneak up on him? Especially across the creaking wood floor.*

"I'm sorry," she said with a smile. "Did I spook you?"

"No," Joe fibbed then turned back to the portrait of a young woman. "Uh, you say she is not the Grey Lady?'

"That's right, Willard Carpenter had another daughter, Louise, who some feel is the Grey Lady, but that's not Louise. That's Louise's sister, Marcia."

"Why isn't there a painting of Louise?" Joe asked.

"No one knows. There is a small portrait of her around that corner."

"Why do they think Louise is the Grey Lady?" Joe followed the lady across the room to look at the portrait of Louise Carpenter. The small portrait hung so high on the wall it was practically obscure. Joe had never given ghost stories any thought, and if asked his opinion of ghosts and spooks he probably would have replied that people who believed in them needed more things to occupy their minds. That, or they were ready for a nice new straight jacket. But he figured there was no harm in listening to the story of Louise Carpenter.

"Louise was the daughter of Willard Carpenter, a wealthy and influential citizen here in Evansville back in the latter part of the nineteenth century. As the story goes, when Willard Carpenter decided to leave the bulk of his money in a trust to build the library, Louise went to court claiming that her father was not mentally competent. She lost the case and with it any claim to her father's money. It's said that Louise Carpenter will haunt this library until it is given back to an heir of the Carpenter family. But that's just the most popular version of who the Grey Lady is. Personally, I don't think Louise is the Grey Lady."

"Oh? Why do you think that?"

"It's said that Louise Carpenter was extremely spoiled and could be a very nasty person when she didn't get her way. Our Grey Lady is a benevolent spirit not fitting with what I've heard about Louise."

"So there are other ideas?" Joe asked.

"A couple of my co-workers believe the Grey Lady is a woman who died in the library in the early days and loved the books so much she never left. Still others believe the ghost has nothing to do with the library but is someone who died a violent death on this land long before the library was built."

"Have you ever seen the ghost?" Joe asked.

"I've never gotten a clear view of her, but a number of times I've caught a moving blur out of the corner of my eye. And one night as I was locking up and on my way out I heard the water faucet in the ladies room come on as I passed by. I went in and turned it off. On my way out of the restroom the faucet came on again, not slowly, but quickly, like when a person turns on a faucet."

"You need to call my dad, he's a plumber." Joe smiled.

"I see you have doubts," the lady said pleasantly.

"I've never thought much about ghosts."

"Neither had I. We didn't call a plumber. Our maintenance man checked the faucet and found nothing wrong with it. But we did eventually bring in a team of ghost researchers."

"You mean like the Ghostbusters?"

"Well, not exactly like the Ghostbusters," she grinned. "This was a team of researchers who travel the country researching claims of paranormal activity. I don't understand much technical jargon, but they talked about something to do with magnetic fields—an anomaly here, an anomaly there that might indicate an unexplained presence."

"Wow, that is weird," Joe said. He was ready to change the subject. Thankfully the lady beat him to it.

"Well, I'm sure you didn't come here to listen to an old lady tell ghost stories. Is there something I can help you with?"

"Uh, yes, thanks. I came in here a couple of years ago and did some research of my family's history for a project in an English class. Now I'm hoping to find some information about a couple of people who lived in Evansville eighty years ago. Things look different in here now and I really don't know where to start."

"Yes, we have many more computers now than we did two years ago. A wider variety of research is accessible through the new computers. Our genealogy department is upstairs. I'll show you."

The lady led the way up the stairs Joe had noticed when he first entered the building. There were several flights, each step creaking. On the wall of the last flight hung a life-sized painting of George Washington and his horse. The decor of another age. Joe felt as if he had traveled back in time.

The second floor was much like the first. The ceilings were as high and the floor-to-ceiling windows were there. Several computers, looking very much out of place in this time warp of a building, sat on tables along a far wall.

"Let's get you set up over here," the lady told Joe as she led him toward some file cabinets and a table that had a huge map of Vanderburgh County under its glass top. Joe draped his letterman jacket over the back of one of the chairs. The lady asked Joe about the names.

"Suda Mae Jackson and Thomas O'Donnell. I don't know his middle name."

"You say they lived in Evansville in the twenties?"

"Yes, I know they were here in 1921."

"Do you know how old they were at that time?"

"They were both in high school. Suda was sixteen. Tommy, or Thomas, was about the same age."

"We'll check birth records first," the lady told Joe.

"I know Suda was born in England, but Thomas was probably born here in Evansville."

"Are these people relatives of yours?"

"No, ma'am. I'm doing this for a project in my social studies class." Joe didn't want to recite the entire story of the diary.

From a nearby file cabinet, the lady picked out a box of microfilm and loaded it into a viewer on the table.

"This box covers 1900 to 1910. If my subtraction is correct, people born during that decade would have been anywhere from eleven years of age to twenty-one in 1921, so that should cover anyone in high school. Anyone born around here during that decade should be listed."

The lady showed Joe how to work the viewing machine which was a simple matter of turning a crank to spin the roll of film. He remembered using these machines two years ago. It took Joe several minutes to spin through the years and the alphabetical lists of people. He went through the "Js" slowly. Joe was not expecting to find Suda's name but he checked nevertheless. He was right. There were many "Jacksons" but no Suda. He spun the film back to 1900 and cranked the handle to the "Os". No "Thomas" turned up that year or the next. Finally the name appeared on the screen. A Thomas Patrick O'Donnell was born on February 25, 1904, to a Shamus and Katherine O'Donnell. This Thomas would have been seventeen in 1921.

"This must be him!" Joe said.

"Good," said the lady. "Now let's see if we can trace them further. Marriage records are on the computer but only people with a library card are allowed to access them. Do you have a card for this library? Regular public library cards won't work."

Joe told the lady he did not have a Willard Library card so they went downstairs and took care of the paperwork. Back upstairs, the lady showed Joe the software for accessing marriage records then she showed him where to find death records, which, like birth information, were on microfilm. He was off to the races. For the marriage records the computer could do the searching through the myriad names and dates. Joe typed in "Thomas Patrick O'Donnell" and clicked on the SEARCH button. In just a few seconds the information appeared on the screen. Thomas Patrick O'Donnell married a Suda Mae Jackson at Saint Boniface Roman Catholic Church on April 24, 1926.

Joe felt the hairs on his neck bristle. He found it eerie uncovering facts about real people who until that moment had seemed more like fictional characters in a novel. By flip-flopping back and forth between microfilm and computerized records, Joe assembled a great deal of information—more than he had expected, and much of it unhappy.

Tommy and Suda had one child, a son born on March 19, 1930, whom they christened Patrick (Tommy's middle name). Joe felt an unexpected and strong feeling of sadness when he went to the microfilm death records and saw that Suda died on March 19, 1930, the same day her son Patrick was born. Tommy died on the same day as Suda but in 1988. He was eighty-four. Patrick, their son, preceded his father in death by two decades. Patrick's date of death was listed as May 12, 1967. He would have been only thirty-seven when he died. Reason for death was listed as "armed conflict" and the place of death Vietnam.

Tommy and Suda's only child was killed in the Vietnam War. Joe wished he wasn't reading some of this and almost stopped there, but a gnawing curiosity pushed him on.

Patrick, Suda's son, married and fathered a daughter. Records showed the daughter, Molly, was born in 1958. Molly O'Donnell married a man named David Sanders on June 13, 1979. The records listed two offspring credited to David and Molly Sanders: a son named Keith, born in 1981; and a daughter named Morgan, born in 1985.

When Joe saw the year 1985 it suddenly occurred to him that this descendant of Tommy and Suda would be about his age. Joe was born in 1984. Morgan should be a high school student, probably a junior or maybe even a senior like Joe, depending on what age she started school.

Morgan Sanders. The name did not ring a bell. He looked up information on Morgan Sanders. She was born at Deaconess Hospital in Evansville and her parents address on the day she was born was on New Harmony Way, a street on the west side of town. If the family still lived in Evansville, and on the west side, Morgan should be a student at Reitz or at Mater Dei High School, a parochial school on that side of town built after WWII.

Joe spent a few minutes trying to find more information on Suda, Tommy, or any of their descendants but found nothing. He printed out copies of the records. The lady who had helped him had since gone to the main floor to work the checkout counter. Joe looked at the clock and was surprised to find he had been at the library for almost two hours. He paid the lady for the photocopies and thanked her for her help. The storm that had been brewing when he pulled into the parking lot was now announcing its presence. Lightning cracked and Joe felt the first few drops of rain as he walked to the truck. The weather matched Joe Rocker's mood. Gloomy.

At home, Joe pulled last year's school yearbook from a shelf and flipped through the pages. Finally, among the photographs of sophomores—she would be a junior now—was the picture of a dark-haired girl named Morgan Sanders.

Chapter 21

As he pulled into the school parking lot Monday morning, Joe's mind was on one thing, well, two things—Suda's diary and the information he had gathered yesterday at Willard Library. The trip to the library strengthened Joe's curiosity and resolve to find out more about the mystery of the diary. Yesterday's detective work revealed that a descendant of Suda and Tommy, a girl who would be a great-granddaughter named Morgan Sanders, attended Reitz High School.

Morgan. Great-granddaughter of Suda. The thought struck Joe that unusual first names for the females must be a family tradition.

Joe parked in his usual spot in the lower lot near the fieldhouse and walked up the steps of Reitz Bowl to the school. Instead of heading to the Link where most of the students congregated before classes started, Joe detoured to the counselor's offices. Joe was greeted by a smile from Mrs. Brown, the ever-cheerful counselor's secretary.

"What's up, Mrs. Brown?"

"Oh, hey Joe. Did you ever give me your senior photo?"

"Uh, I forgot. I'll bring it tomorrow," Joe promised. "Hey, Mrs. Brown, can I look up something in the student schedules?" Joe worked in the office during a free period and was familiar with the schedule book.

"You know where it is. Just make sure you're not late for class."

Joe went to the teacher's assistant table and opened the thick, blue book. Inside were the schedules for every student in the school. Joe turned to the "S" section.

"Sanders, Morgan. Sanders, Morgan," Joe muttered to himself as he looked. "Here it is!" Joe said out loud. Mrs. Brown and the other students in the room turned to look at him. Joe ignored the stares, happy he had found the name. Joe knew he had no classes with this person, but from the schedule book he found out that they shared the same lunch period.

Joe thanked Mrs. Brown who was busy with a long line of students who were requesting to see their counselors—each with a dire emergency and each expecting Mrs. Brown to get them taken care of before the bell rang in five minutes. Joe waved to Mrs. Brown on his way out.

"Have a good day, Joe," said Mrs. Brown. "And don't forget that photo."

"Okay, class, just leave your stuff where it is and we'll continue after lunch," Mr. Kern yelled above the sounds of folding papers and sixty fast-moving feet.

Finally it was time for lunch. Joe had "B" lunch period which meant he went to half of his math class, then to lunch, then back to the same class for the second half of math. Rushing down the hallway and through the Link, Joe's head ached from a mixture of calculus and thoughts about what he was going to say to Morgan Sanders. He wanted to find out more about Suda, but he did not know this Morgan Sanders, and he was a little worried about how to approach her about her family. After going through the slow-moving lunch line, Joe sat at his usual table with his friends. Most were teammates on the football team who Joe had played football with since elementary school.

"Hey, it's the famous Joe Rocker," Zach Stratton mumbled through his mash potato-filled mouth.

"What's up, girls," Joe said to the all male group. Everyone in the group went out of their way to insult the others whenever possible.

"What takes you so long to get here, Rocker?" asked Tim Grainger. "What do you do, stop in the Link and sign autographs for the little freshmen girls?"

The others at the table laughed.

"The only reason you guys get here before I do is you have Strength and Conditioning class in the Fieldhouse and Coach has to let you out a couple minutes before the bell rings. Then you idiots run up here so you can be the first in line. I have calculus."

"Calculus, that has to bite," said Rick Turner as he filled his mouth with French fries.

"Hey, Rocker, why weren't you down at West Terrace yesterday?" Tim Grainger asked. "Sam Donovan juked Stratton out bad. It was pitiful."

"It wasn't like that," Zach Stratton interjected immediately. "The field was wet and I slipped."

"Yeah, right!" Grainger replied with a snicker.

A dozen or so of the guys always got together on Sundays—their only day off from football practice—to play a little backyard football at West Terrace Elementary School. It was a convenient place to play with plenty of well-kept grassy areas.

"You know I believe you, Zach," Joe said tongue-in-cheek. The others bellowed knowing Joe was ribbing Stratton.

"You suck, Rocker," Zach said when he figured out Joe was not sincere. They all laughed again before Joe changed the subject.

"Hey, guys, you remember me telling you about that old diary I found a couple of weeks ago? The one written by a girl who went to school here back in the twenties."

A couple of the guys shrugged like they did not remember. Rick Turner said, "Yeah, so what?"

"I went to Willard Library yesterday to look up some stuff. That's why I wasn't at West Terrace. I went through a ton of records, and it took awhile, but I did find out some things."

"Like what?" asked Rick. "The girl's phone number? I know you haven't had a girlfriend since you and Christie split up, but don't you think the girl who wrote that diary would be a little old for you, Rocker?"

A couple of the guys chuckled but Joe ignored them.

"I think there is a girl going to school here now who is a descendant of the girl in the diary. She would be a great-granddaughter. Her name is Morgan Sanders. Do any of you guys know her?"

Rick Turner and Zach Stratton shook their heads. Tim Grainger spoke up.

"Yeah, I know her," said Tim. "She's in my English class."

"What's she like," Joe asked quickly.

"She's out there, man. A real freak. Black nail polish, black lipstick, and more piercings than General Custer after Sitting Bull got finished with him. She doesn't socialize with anyone, not even other freaks from what I can see. The only person I've ever seen her talk to—besides a teacher when she has to—is Brent Hunter. She carries around this bag of trinkets and is always messing around with the stuff in that bag."

Great! thought Joe. *Just my luck.*

"I looked up her schedule and it said she has lunch this period," Joe said. "Do you see her in here now, Tim?"

"Won't be hard to spot her if she is in here," Grainger said. The big tight end stood and scanned the cafeteria for a long moment. "Nope, don't see her." He sat back down and resumed eating.

"Hey," said Rick, "did you say she hangs out with Brent Hunter?"

"Yeah," Tim answered while chewing an apple. "At least he's the only one I've ever seen her hang with."

"Last week I got called to the library during lunch because of an overdue book," Rick turned to Joe. "I saw Hunter sitting in there with a girl. It has to be her—a real freak, just like Tim said."

"I wonder if they're up there now?" Joe asked, not expecting anyone to know the answer. "I think I'll head up there and check it out. See you guys at practice," he said as he stood and grabbed his tray.

"Be careful you don't get rabies," Rick joked.

"Yeah," Zach added, "or better take some garlic and a crucifix to protect yourself from Vampira."

Joe left his buddies and headed to the front of the cafeteria. He dumped his trash and put the tray on a nearby stack of many. He knew a pass was required to go to the library during lunch, but he spotted Mrs. Settle, the principal, talking to one of the teachers supervising the doorway. Joe decided to try his luck. Mrs. Settle was tough when it came to school rules, but she would work with any student who had a bonafide request and who approached her about it the right way. Without going into great detail, Joe stressed the history project aspect, and received permission to go to the library.

The library was a comfortable place on the second floor with soft, overstuffed chairs and floor-to-ceiling windows on two sides of the room. One set of windows looked down on the football field in Reitz Bowl; the opposite windows provided a wide vista of the mighty Ohio River and the woods and farmland of Kentucky. Joe signed in and said hello to Mr. Hammonds who was in charge of the library.

It took only a moment to locate Brent Hunter. He sat at a table near the door—alone. Joe walked up to the table.

"Brent, my name is Joe Rocker. How's it going?"

"Okay." Brent turned toward Joe's voice. Brent was blind.

"Some friends told me you might know a girl I'm looking for."

"Yeah? What's her name?"

"Morgan Sanders."

"Yes, I know her. She's around here somewhere. We're studying together; she went to find a book we need."

"She's right behind you." It was a female voice. Joe turned around. She was very pale, a sharp contrast to her jet hair. Each ear sported three or four earrings and a small nose ring adorned her right nostril. The lipstick was not black today, but a dark purple. Heavy black eyeliner turned up at the corners, giving her almost an oriental look. Red lettering on a black t-shirt read *I'm looking at dumb people.*

"Uh, hi, I'm Joe Rocker."

"I know who you are. You're Mr. Big Shot Football Hero. We've met already. Don't you remember?"

"Uh . . ."

"Oh come now. Surely you remember. You were so gallant. You opened the door for me one day in the counselor's office."

Joe remembered. She was the girl who had been leaning against the door and fell when he opened it.

"Sorry about that. I didn't know you were leaning against the door. I didn't recognize you because your hair was pink then . . . wasn't it?"

"So what? Tomorrow it might be green."

Joe stood there not knowing what to say—one of those awkward moments.

"So, why are you looking for me?" she asked.

"Uh, it's kind of a long story. Can we sit down?"

She shrugged. "It's a free country." She sat down at the table next to Brent. Joe sat across from them.

"I was working with my dad in an old house down on Wabash Avenue, ripping a wall out for a remodeling job, and I found an old diary from the 1920s. It is the diary of a teenage girl named Suda Mae Jackson. Have you ever heard of her?"

"No."

"How about the name Tommy O'Donnell?"

"No."

"You've never heard of those names?" Joe had hoped she would be able to tell him something about Suda and Tommy, but the air was rapidly going out of that balloon.

"No, O'Donnell is my mother's maiden name, but I've never heard of your Tommy."

"What was your grandfather's first name?"

"Patrick, why?"

Joe dug in his backpack and found the photocopies from Willard Library.

"Here it is," Joe said excitedly. He showed her the paper and pointed. "Patrick. He was the only child of Thomas and Suda O'Donnell. Tommy and Suda O'Donnell are your great-grandparents. It is your great-grandmother's diary that I found."

Morgan's look was a combination of curiosity and suspicion. She didn't know quite what to think of this jock and his story. She had little time for jocks, especially football players. From what she had seen, football players spent most of their time scratching their rear ends and playing practical jokes on each other.

"So what's in this diary?" she asked cautiously.

"A lot." Joe again reached into his backpack, this time producing the diary. Reluctantly he handed it to her. It was a spur of the moment decision and giving away the diary was not easy. The diary had been his bond to Suda. "Here, take it. You should have it."

"You're giving it to me?" She looked at him strangely.

"Your great-grandmother wrote it. I know she would rather her great-granddaughter have it than me. But I would like to find out more about a few things she wrote about in the diary. After you read it, you'll know what I mean. Will you look me up after you've finished reading it?"

She looked first at him, then at the diary. "I guess so."

"I know you probably think all this is weird, but you'll see why I'm curious about your great-grandparents. Some pages are missing. Like I said, you'll see what I mean after you read it."

"Okay, if you say so."

Joe picked up his backpack and left the library.

Brent Hunter, who had sat quietly listening to the exchange, now spoke: "Well, open it up, Morgan, and read me a little of it, if I'm not being too nosy."

Morgan opened the old diary. She carefully flipped through a few pages before turning back to the first page and reading aloud.

Diary of Suda Mae Jackson

Friday, 10 June 1921

I dreamt last night, me first night aboard this ship, that me mum and I were together once again. In the dream it was years later from yesterday when we said goodbye on the dock in Portsmouth. Years later, but she had not changed, and she wore the same grey clothes she wore when we waved goodbye as the ship pulled away. I am wondering if me dream will come true. I am wondering if I will ever see me mum again.

Chapter 22

"Good morning Evansville, you're listening to WIKY-104.1 FM."

Morgan Sanders hated to be awakened by nerve-grating sound of an alarm clock buzzer, so, on school days, she sat her clock to the WIKY Morning Show with Dennis Jon Bailey and Diane Douglas. Morgan rolled over, reached out, and, after some sleepy-eyed fumbling in the dark, found the switch on her bedside table lamp. Normally Morgan remained in bed for several minutes, putting off arising as long as possible, but this morning, even though Morgan had not fallen asleep until almost 2:30 a.m., she immediately sat up on the edge of the bed.

The abbreviated sleep was the result of reading the diary Joe Rocker had given her yesterday at school. According to Joe Rocker, it was the diary of her great-grandmother. Last night Morgan read it straight through—twice.

Morgan lived with her mother in a two bedroom flat off Maryland Street. Originally built during World War II to help house the enormous number of out-of-towners who descended on Evansville for the well-paying wartime factory jobs, the barracks-looking structures had been remodeled several times and were now one and two bedroom apartments. The rent was cheap.

A brother, Keith, was in the Army and stationed in Germany. Since Keith left two years ago, it was now just Morgan and her mother.

Morgan's father had blown town when Morgan was three. He called a couple times a year from California, sometime around Morgan's birthday and usually around Christmas. Morgan had not seen him in three years. Then for a few years during elementary school Morgan had a stepfather. For a while family life chugged along halfway smoothly, but when Morgan was in the sixth grade, her mother and stepfather separated.

Her mother took back her maiden name, O'Donnell, and seemed intent to make her second failure at marriage her last. She did this by avoiding men and relationships altogether, evidently determined to remain single for the rest of her life. Financially, life was never easy. Morgan's mother worked on the assembly line at a factory that made refrigerators. The pay was decent but life was lived paycheck to paycheck—never anything left after the bills were paid. A savings account was a pipe dream.

Morgan and her mother were close, but because they shared several personality traits, a prominent one an innate stubbornness, conflicts sometimes arose.

"I got up at two o'clock last night and noticed the light still on in your room," Molly O'Donnell commented as she set a donut on the table for Morgan. Morgan checked for milk, but they were out again.

"I was reading," Morgan said as she grabbed a Diet Coke out of the refrigerator.

"I can see it wasn't a fashion magazine."

"That's funny, Mom. Why are you always riding me about what I wear?" Morgan's camouflage jeans were tucked into black combat boots. She had on a bright yellow men's long sleeved shirt that was not tucked into the pants and a candy cane striped men's necktie. Her hair had the look of recent electric shock.

"I'm your mother, that's why. It's my job."

"It's your job to nag me to death?"

"Don't be a smart-aleck, Morgan Sanders. You would be such a pretty girl if you didn't dress and wear your makeup like you were auditioning for the *Rocky Horror Picture Show."*

Morgan knew that when her mother put her first and last name together an argument brewed. Morgan was in no mood for a verbal boxing match this morning. She had other things on her mind, so she sought to change the subject.

"Mom, tell me again about your dad, my Grandpa Patrick." Morgan had heard the stories about her grandfather serving with distinction but dying in Vietnam in the sixties; she had seen his medals which her mom kept safely stored in the top of her closet. But now she wanted to hear it again. Her mom looked at her for a moment before speaking.

"Your grandfather was a hero in Vietnam. He was a captain in the

Rangers and was wounded saving some of his men. He died from the wounds two days later." Morgan's mother's voice had lost its confrontational edge when she talked about her father.

"What do you remember about him?"

"I was only nine when he died. He was a career Army man so we moved a lot. He was a big, strong, handsome man as you can see in the pictures. He used to pick me up like I was weightless and twirl me over his head. I would sit for hours in his lap, eventually falling asleep. He would carry me to my room and tuck me in. When I was very small—four or five—I wouldn't go to sleep until Daddy tucked me in."

"How about his father?" Morgan continued probing.

"My grandfather?" Morgan's mom paused for a moment before continuing. "Well, my dad got his good looks from him. Grandpa Thomas, your great-grandfather, died when you were about three. You won't remember him, of course, but he used to sit and rock you for hours. He always liked to say that you were the spitting image of his wife."

The last statement hit Morgan like a thunderbolt. More than a slight shiver went down her spine. It was more like a major tremor.

"What did you say?" Morgan asked.

"I said your great-grandfather always commented on how much you looked like his wife."

"What do we know about her?"

"She died very young—giving birth to my father. Grandpa Thomas would talk about her for hours. He had some great stories about her. She was born in England."

If Morgan had any doubts that the Suda Jackson of the diary was her great-grandmother, they were now gone. Her mother continued.

"Grandpa Thomas never remarried. Their's was quite a love story. I always felt sorry for Grandpa Thomas in some ways. His wife dying so young, then having to bury their only child—no one should have to bury one of their children. Grandpa Thomas was always ready for a little fun and mischief. He always had a twinkle in his eye, but at the same time I felt there was always a great sadness there too."

"I never told you this," Morgan's mom continued, "but when Grandpa Thomas was diagnosed with cancer, he was given only three months to live. He fought through terrible pain to stay alive for seven months—several months longer than any of the doctors said he would live. His one wish was to die on the same day his wife died, which, of course, was also his dead son's birthday. He was totally blind and out of his head with pain the last couple of weeks, even morphine wasn't helping. Anytime someone would enter his hospital room he would ask them if it was March 19th yet. Finally, on March 19th, I was sitting in a chair by his bed. He asked and I told him the date. It wasn't long before he opened his eyes. You know how you can look into a blind person's eyes and tell they're blind? That's the way Grandpa Thomas's eyes had looked for weeks. But now when he opened his eyes, the old twinkle was back. They were not the eyes of a blind man. It looked like he was looking at someone standing on the other side of his bed. He said 'Suda,' his wife's name, then he closed his eyes and died peacefully."

For a long moment nothing more was said. Morgan sat silently, taking in the poignant story of an elderly widower holding on to the love for a wife he had lost over a half century before. Morgan tried to imagine the elderly Grandpa Thomas as the young man of Suda's diary—Tommy O'Donnell.

"Do we have any pictures of Grandpa Thomas?" Morgan asked.

"There's a few in a one of the old albums in the hallway closet. But you'll be late for school."

"I have time, Mom." Morgan left the kitchen and retrieved the albums. Back in the kitchen she flipped through one of the albums while her mom looked in another. Molly O'Donnell stopped, pointed to a photograph on one of the pages, and turned the album toward her daughter.

"Here's a picture of Grandpa Thomas, your great-grandfather, rocking you to sleep."

Morgan stopped and looked anxiously. In the photograph a distinguished looking, neatly dressed old man sat holding and smiling at an infant in his arms. Morgan now remembered seeing this photograph years ago but until now it had meant little to her.

"I don't guess we would have any pictures of him when he was younger," Morgan asked, "or pictures of his wife."

"There's an old wedding photo of them buried somewhere in the footlocker in my bedroom closet."

"A picture of Tommy and Suda???" Morgan almost shouted it, startling her mother.

"What's gotten in to you? Why all this interest in your family tree all of a sudden? And why do you call Grandpa Thomas 'Tommy?'"

"A dumb jock at school found an old diary written by Suda O'Donnell—her last name was Jackson then. She wrote the diary when she was a teenager, before she married Tommy—Grandpa Thomas."

"What?" Morgan's mother said incredulously. "Where did he find that?"

"He said he was working with his dad on an old house on Wabash and found it when he tore down a wall or something."

"Where is this diary?"

"In my room."

"Let me see it."

"I'll get the diary," Morgan told her mom, "while you find that wedding picture."

Morgan raced to her room and grabbed the diary. Molly O'Donnell went to her bedroom and began uncovering an old trunk buried in the back of her closet under blankets and boxes of Christmas decorations.

"Here it is, Mom." Morgan handed the diary to her mother.

Molly O'Donnell temporarily stopped what she was doing and carefully thumbed through her grandmother's diary. She handed the diary back to Morgan with intentions of reading it that evening, then pulled the trunk from the closet.

The trunk had not been opened in years and the latches took some jimmying. Finally the lid opened. On top was Molly's wedding dress; underneath the dress were assorted mementos of family life: high school diplomas, birth certificates, and baby shoes. Molly held up Morgan's First Communion dress. A cigar box of very old photographs was found near the bottom. Some of the folks pictured Morgan's mother recognized and some had names and dates handwritten on the backs. Many of the old photos were unmarked and the people's names long forgotten.

Under the cigar box was a 5" x 7" sepia wedding photo in a heavy metal frame.

"Here it is," Molly O'Donnell announced. "It's a picture of Grandpa Thomas and his wife, Suda, on their wedding day. Morgan's mother held the picture to the light. Morgan saw her mother's face turn ashen.

"Oh, my gosh."

"What's wrong, Mom?"

"I, uh . . . I haven't looked at this picture since you were a baby." Molly O'Donnell was visibly shaken.

"So, let me see it."

Molly looked at Morgan, almost as if she wasn't sure she wanted her daughter to see the photograph. Slowly she handed Morgan the picture of Thomas O'Donnell and his bride. In the picture a tall, handsome young man stood grinning with his arm around a pretty young woman in a white wedding dress with a smile only brides have on their wedding day.

Morgan gazed into the face of Suda Mae O'Donnell née Jackson.

The face Morgan saw was her own.

Chapter 23

"This is a picture of you," Joe told Morgan.

"It's not me!" Morgan almost shouted as she sat with Joe Rocker at a table near the back of the school cafeteria. She had brought the wedding picture of Tommy and Suda to school to show him and now regretted it. An image in a seventy-five-year-old photograph had unnerved Morgan that morning. Now, visibly shaken by Joe's comment, Morgan grabbed the picture out of his hands and put it back in her backpack.

"The girl in the photo has no nose ring or hair that looks like a rat's nest, but besides that she looks just like you," said Joe, making things worse.

"How would you know? You've been playing football so long your brains are freakin' Jello!"

"What does that mean?" Joe didn't like dumb jock comments.

"You know it's not me. It's my great-grandmother, Suda O'Donnell."

Joe could see Morgan was upset and decided to back off. "Has your mom read the diary?"

"Not yet. She plans on doing that tonight." There was a short pause before Morgan asked, "What do you think happened to them? With the Ku Klux Klan trouble I mean."

"I don't know," Joe said, "but we have to find out."

"Maybe there are more pages still in that wall where you found the diary."

"Nope. I've already been back and checked in the wall and looked around the entire house—twice."

"Well, we know the pages were torn out on purpose," said Morgan.

"How do we know that?" Joe asked.

"You can tell they were ripped out at the same time." Morgan opened the dairy to the spot of the missing pages. "The material on the inside of the spine is yellow with age—the same as the remaining pages. If the pages fell out years later, I think it would look different. Plus, all the pages still in the book are secure, none are loose. Besides the yellowing, the diary is in excellent shape. If age had made the missing pages fall out, why would the remaining pages be so secure?"

Joe didn't say it but he was impressed with Morgan's detective skills.

"But how sure are we that more of the story is missing?" said Joe. "Maybe, because of all the bad things happening, Suda just decided to stop writing."

"Then why the missing pages?" Morgan shot back.

"I don't know," said Joe. "Hey, don't get mad, I'm just playing devil's advocate here. Maybe she used the rest of the pages, a few at a time, for other things—homework or something. She complains in the diary about the high price of paper."

Neither of them believed that theory accounted for the missing pages, not even Joe who added, "Like I said, we have to find out. What do we do next?"

"I've never been to the graves, but my mom told me this morning that Grandpa Thomas—Tommy—and Suda are buried in Saint Joseph Cemetery."

"Sounds like that's the next stop," Joe said. "It will have to wait till this weekend. By the time football practice ends, it's dark. If you'll give me your address and phone, I'll call you this weekend." Joe paused for a moment before asking: "Are you coming to the game Friday?"

"Of course not."

Chapter 24

This November night was cold but clear. And the bruising battle under the lights of Reitz Bowl was now in the fourth quarter. That the game was especially brutal came as no surprise. When Reitz played Castle, it could be no other way. The Castle Knights, like Reitz, boasted a proud football tradition. Both teams were well-coached; players on both teams took their football seriously; both squads were prepared well in practice, watching hours of film of each opponent; and players from both schools worked hard in the weightroom year round.

Adding to each team's incentive was the fact that this game was for the sectional championship. The winners advanced to the regional; the losers turned in their equipment, their season over.

Reitz drew first blood in the second quarter when Tim Grainger caught a pass, eluded a tackler, and managed to stretch the ball over the goal line after a hit by a pair of Castle defenders. Unfortunately, on the ensuing kickoff, Castle ran the ball back to the Reitz 25 yard line. Castle's good field position made it tough on the Reitz defense. Castle ended up in the Reitz endzone five plays later and the score was tied. Right before the first half ended, Reitz managed to get close enough for a field goal, so the Panthers took a precarious three point lead to the lockerroom.

The Knights went up by four points early in the third quarter thanks to a heady play by a Castle cornerback. Timing his move, the Knight defender stepped in front of a Reitz receiver, intercepted the ball, and cruised into the Reitz endzone.

Later in the third period another turnover led to a score, but this time Castle was the victim. A blitz was called and Joe Rocker hammered the Castle quarterback as he attempted a handoff. The ball squirted free. Big Daddy Grabowski, a Reitz defensive tackle, fell on the ball at the Castle 24 yard line.

Arnold "Big Daddy" Grabowski was a legend on the team. Big Daddy weighed 290 pounds and was known far and wide for the incredible amounts of food he could consume. A fight with some high school bullies when Big Daddy was in middle school cost him four upper front teeth. He wore a partial plate in civilian life, but removed it for football. Big Daddy's parents abandoned him when he was three. He lived with his grandmother in a rundown apartment. Big Daddy struggled mightily with his grades, but he loved football so much he worked hard to maintain his eligibility. Joe figured if it were not for football, Big Daddy would have dropped out of school his sophomore year.

Big Daddy had tremendous upper body strength and one of his specialities, besides eating barbecued ribs, was coming up with fumbled footballs, especially at the bottom of a pile up.

After Big Daddy's fumble recovery, the determined Panther offense took the field and capitalized on the break in three plays. The touchdown came when Antwain Davis ran a counter play off tackle and scored from 12 yards out.

So that is where the teams stood as the fourth quarter began—Reitz holding a small lead, 17 to 14.

The fourth quarter proved to be a duel between punters. Each team's defense had proved tough all night and coaches now elected to play a careful game of field position. The coaches were gambling that the other team would make a mistake. The mistake came with two minutes left in the game, and Joe Rocker made it.

The Knights had managed to work their way to midfield, but now they faced a fourth down and six yards to go for a first down. With time running out on the Knights, they were forced to go for a first down instead of punt. If Reitz held here, the Panther offense would take the field and run out the clock.

The Knights had all their timeouts left, so they did not have to pass every down. Joe knew this and was not surprised when the Knights' quarterback took the snap and pitched the ball to their tailback on a sweep. The Castle runner wanted to make sure he picked up enough yards for the first down then get out of bounds to stop the clock and preserve a time out. Joe fought through a blocker, then sprinted toward the sideline and the Castle runningback.

Rick Turner, the outside linebacker on the sweep side, managed to string out the play and force the Castle ballcarrier to run wider before turning up the field. This allowed Joe to be in position to make the tackle before the Castle player picked up the critical six yards. Nearing the sideline, Joe thought the Castle player would lower his shoulder and try to dive for a first down. Running full tilt, Joe steeled himself for the hit. But the Castle player's foot stepped out of bounds before the impact. Joe delivered a tremendous hit and drove the runningback out of bounds and into a crowd of Castle players and coaches who immediately screamed for an unnecessary roughness call. A referee, perhaps influenced more by the fit from the Castle sideline than what he actually saw, threw the flag.

So instead of Reitz taking over and running out the clock, the Knights had a first down and the ball fifteen yards closer to the Panther's goal line, putting the ball on the Panther 35 yard line.

This reprieve fired up the Knights' offense and swung the momentum in their favor. Two running plays and two timeouts later the Knights were on the Reitz 17 yard line. The Castle quarterback threw an incomplete pass, then tried a quarterback draw that gained nothing, the tackle made by Joe and Big Daddy at the line of scrimmage. The Reitz defense had once again showed why it led the league in most defensive stats. With time running out, the Knights were forced to take their last timeout. Joe hoped they would go for the endzone but the Castle coach was too smart for that. He sent in his All-Conference kicker who booted the thirty-three yard field goal right through the middle of the goal posts. The score was tied with three seconds on the clock.

Castle squibbed the kickoff, and Reitz was forced to simply fall on the ball as time ran out.

Overtime.

During the short break before overtime, Joe's teammates tried to console him about the penalty but Joe was in no mood to hear sideline platitudes.

"Keep your head up, Joe," Greg Mofield, one of the offensive linemen, told Joe.

"I've got my head up," Joe shouted back. "Stay out of my face!"

An assistant coach overheard the exchange and hurried over. "Calm down, Rocker. We've got work to do."

In overtime, each team got an offensive possession and four downs from the opponent's ten yard line. Whoever scored the most points won the game. If neither team scored, or the overtime ended in another tie, overtime repeated itself until there was a winner.

The coaches huddled with their units while Joe led the other Reitz captains out on the field for the coin toss. Castle won the toss and elected to go on defense.

On first down the Reitz fullback bulled into a tough Castle front for two yards. The next play was a pass. Kevin Harper, the Reitz quarterback, looked for Tim Grainger in the endzone. Grainger stretched out in full flight but only brushed the ball with his fingertips.

Incomplete.

On third down, Harper took the snap and dropped back for another pass. Antwain Davis brush-blocked a hard charging defensive end, then sneaked out into the right flat that had been cleared by a Reitz receiver who took the Castle cornerback away from the action. The cornerback was playing man-to-man defense so it was a simple matter of running the Castle player into the endzone.

Kevin Harper hit Davis perfectly and Davis outran a linebacker to the endzone, diving across the goal line just inside the orange marker.

Touchdown!

The Reitz fans went wild.

The crowd's joy was dampened, however, when a low snap caused a poor hold and the extra point was missed. Reitz was ahead by six points, but now Castle would go on offense. Everyone realized the missed extra point could doom the Panthers. Castle's highly touted placekicker, who had already kicked a 33-yard fieldgoal, had never missed an extra point. If the Knights scored, an easy extra point—practically automatic for Castle—would win them the game.

And Joe Rocker would bear the blame. Not so much in other

people's eyes as in his own. Even though watching film later would reveal the penalty on Joe at the end of the fourth quarter was extremely questionable, he would blame himself for the loss. Not until the penalty did it really hit him that this might be his last game as a Panther. His last game in Reitz Bowl. His last time to wear the silver helmet. Joe's father had played for Reitz, and his grandfather. Both were in the stands along with the rest of his family. His 9-year-old cousin, who dreamed (like Joe had dreamed when he was little) that one day he would wear the silver helmet, was in the stands.

Joe Rocker was on a mission. He owed this one to his family and to the Reitz football tradition that he had been taught to respect.

Rocker led the defense onto the field. The team huddled and Joe called the defense, but before they broke the huddle Joe spoke to his teammates.

"Listen up!" Joe was shouting. "We've all been together for a long time and put in a lot of work to be here. This isn't going to be our last game! Everybody here is going to leave everything they have on the field! Everyone fly to the ball except you backside contain guys—if you have backside contain keep your eyes open, they're liable to try some counters or just cut the ball back if nothing is open! Lots of helmets on the ball! Let's go!"

FIRST DOWN.

The huge Castle offensive linemen took their places. The Reitz defensive linemen quickly lined up on them. Because of the temperature, the breath of the linemen on both teams could be seen coming through their helmet face masks.

Castle's first play was a run off tackle. The Knight tailback lost a yard, buried under a swarm of angry young men in silver helmets.

SECOND DOWN.

Still convinced they could run the ball behind their big offensive line, Castle called on their fullback. It was a trap play. At the snap, Joe saw the Castle guard directly in front of him pull down the line. Joe was too quick for the blocker assigned to fill for the pulling guard. He shot through the hole and followed the guard who led him to the ballcarrier.

The collision could be heard in the stands. Both Joe and the fullback were slow getting up. It was another one yard loss for the Knights.

Joe's vision was blurry as he returned to the huddle. Rick Turner noticed something was wrong.

"Rocker, are you okay?"

"Yeah, just give me a second." Joe bent over, put his hands on his knees and shook some of the cobwebs.

"Great hit, man," Big Daddy said to Joe.

THIRD DOWN.

Nick Jensen, the Castle quarterback, spun and stepped toward the tailback in a repeat of their first down play. The tailback was again swarmed under. But this time the quarterback had faked the handoff and kept the ball, spinning and heading in the opposite direction. The play was a bootleg and the quarterback had the option of passing or running the ball. The number one receiver was the tight end who had dragged over the middle of the field. But Pete Younger, one of the Reitz safeties, had the tight end covered, so the quarterback ran the ball. As soon as he crossed the line of scrimmage, the Panther defensive backs abandoned their coverages and closed quickly on the quarterback, but not before he made his way to the three yard line. The ball was placed down on the left hash mark.

FOURTH DOWN.

The long, bruising game between the two proud teams had now come down to one play. Castle used a timeout. Joe and the other defensive players jogged to the sideline to talk things over with the coaches.

"They've had no success at running inside the tackles," Coach Hart told the players. His voice was coarse and scratchy from nearly three hours of yelling from the sidelines. "And they haven't thrown the ball from inside the five all season. They're going to try to outrun us to the perimeter."

"Rockfish," Coach Hart said to Joe. Coach had nicknames for everyone, most made sense only to him. Joe's nickname came from an old television show Coach watched in his younger days.

"Yeah, Coach."

"Watch number 62. Remember what we talked about this week in practice. He's their quickest lineman and pulls on sweeps. The ball is on the left hash, but that doesn't mean they will go to the wide side of the field. They might attack the short side. If they try the short side, they'll try to crack Turnip (Rick Turner) with the split end." Then Coach turned to Turner: "Turnip, keep your eyes open for the crack from the wide out. Don't get cracked and let the guy outside and one-on-one with our corner. Turn him inside where your help is."

"Right, Coach," said Turner.

"Okay, men," Coach said, "let's stop them here and get this thing over with."

Some of the players took a last swig of water from the squeeze bottles, then the defense returned to the field.

High up in the Reitz Bowl pressbox, a radio announcer was ready to resume broadcasting after a commercial break during the Castle timeout.

"Welcome back, ladies and gentlemen. The teams have retaken the field and are huddling up. We are in overtime. The Reitz Panthers are trying to hold on to a six point lead and advance to next week's regional. It's a lead that is in great jeopardy at this moment. It is fourth down for the Castle Knights. The ball sits on the left hash at the Reitz three yard line. A great ball game between two fine teams comes down to this.

The Knights break the huddle . . . Jensen looks over the Reitz defense and puts his hands under center . . . the snap! . . . Jensen pitches to the halfback, Broshier! . . . it's a sweep around left end! . . . Broshier turns up and lowers his shoulder for the endzone! . . . oh, my goodness! Broshier is hammered at the two yard line by Rocker! . . . the ball is on the ground and bouncing into the endzone! . . . there is a tremendous pile up!

Ladies and gentlemen, the officials are trying to unpile the players! It's pandemonium in the endzone! Castle players are trying to pull Reitz players off the pile. The Reitz players seem in no hurry to unpile. Officials are trying to control the situation. The winning team will be the one who comes out of the pile with the football—if it's Castle, they'll need an extra point, but that's pretty much a gimme for them. This game has been a defensive struggle and it looks like it will end, one way or another, on a tremendous defensive play by the Reitz middle linebacker Joe Rocker. Rocker put a tremendous hit on Tyrone Broshier, the Castle ballcarrier. Broshier is still on the ground at the two yard line. It is the second fumble Rocker has forced in this game . . . Hold on . . . Reitz players are jumping up and down in the endzone! . . . a Reitz player is standing and holding the ball over his head! . . . it's number 79, Arnold "Big Daddy" Grabowski! Reitz students are draining out of the stands and running onto the field. . . ."

At the top of the Bowl, far to one end, Morgan Sanders sat watching.

Chapter 25

Morgan Sanders sat in Joe Rocker's pickup as he turned off of Maryland Street. It was early Sunday afternoon and he had just picked her up at her apartment.

"So, I hear you were quite the hero Friday night," Morgan did not tell Joe she attended the game, and she did not wait for a response to her comment. "How was your football practice today?"

Joe looked at her. "We don't practice on Sunday," he said cautiously. So far the only comments concerning football he had heard from this girl had been sarcastic ones. "We have to travel to Bloomington Friday for the regional. The coaches are making sure everyone is working hard. Are you coming to the game?"

"Who me? No. I've never been to a football game." Morgan lied, although the Castle game had been her first.

"You've never been to a game? Even a Reitz game in the Bowl?" Joe must have sounded incredulous.

"That's right. Do you find that surprising?"

"Why haven't you ever been to a game?"

"I've never had the urge to watch a bunch of drooling, testosterone-stoked morons beat each other's brains out."

Joe did not want to argue with her and, almost surprising himself, he played her comment for comedy.

"Hey, I resent that remark," Joe sounded serious. "Our whole team has been tested. Only fifty percent of our players are officially morons. The rest have been classified as only slightly stupid."

She looked at him then turned away and looked out the passenger door window. Joe had a feeling she was smiling but she didn't want him to see.

"You should try to make it to Bloomington," Joe suggested. "They have a fan bus, only costs five bucks plus the price of a ticket."

Joe turned off Mesker Park Drive into Saint Joseph Cemetery. The gunmetal sky promised rain and a stiff breeze blew leaves across the narrow asphalt drive in front of the truck. He pulled over and stopped in front of a building that looked like a maintenance shed. A large garage door was open and inside an old man worked on the engine of a small tractor. Joe and Morgan got out of the truck and approached the old man.

"Sir," said Joe, "we're looking for a grave. Can you help us?"

The old man did not look up and seemed irked at the distraction from the work in front of him. "There's a map in the office."

"Can you point us to the office?" Morgan asked. They had not seen a building that looked like an office on their way in.

"That way." The old man pointed. Joe and Morgan turned back to the truck. "What's the name on the grave?" the old man asked gruffly. Still he had not looked up from his work.

"Thomas O'Donnell," Morgan answered. No response. "His wife, Suda, should be buried here too."

Suddenly the old man stopped working and turned toward the two young people.

"Suda? I know that grave," the old man said. "It's in Sector 23." The old man pointed a different direction now. "Over that hill. You'll see the sign for Sector 23. She's in the second row past the big oak tree."

Back in the truck, Joe turned it around and headed in the direction given them.

"I wonder why he knows about my great-grandmother's grave?" Morgan wondered aloud. "This is a big cemetery. There must be thousands of graves here."

Joe looked at her. He could see she was nervous. "He's probably the groundskeeper," Joe tried to calm her. "The old coot's probably been around here since the Civil War. I imagine he knows most of the graves."

"He didn't know Thomas.'"

"Suda is an unusual name," Joe said. "That's probably why he remembered it."

Joe spotted the *Sector 23* sign. A big oak tree sat a couple hundred feet farther down the drive. He parked the truck near the tree. Joe was going to suggest that he start at one end of a row and Morgan the other and walk back and forth until one of them found the graves, but when Morgan stepped out of the truck, she walked, without looking at names on the markers, directly to a spot about half way down a long row of graves. Joe followed. Morgan suddenly stopped and turned toward a gravestone.

✞
Suda Mae O'Donnell
b. Feb. 16, 1905
d. May 19, 1930
Dear and Beloved Wife

Suda's grave was in the middle of three O'Donnell graves. Tommy lay next to Suda. His stone much newer, he not having joined his wife until 1988. On the other side of Suda was the marker for Patrick, Tommy and Suda's only child and Morgan's grandfather. Suda lost her life giving birth to Patrick.

Joe and a very pale Morgan stood in silence for a long time.

Something else brought attention to Suda's grave. A large arrangement of yellow roses in a metal vase adorned the grave. Morgan reached down and pulled out one of the flowers. She felt the petals and placed it to her nose. It was real—and fresh.

Joe finally broke the silence.

"It's sad when you think of them from the diary . . . people our age. Then to stand here at their graves. . . ."

Morgan did not respond to his comments. She replaced the flower in the vase.

"Let's go, Joe."

They got back to the truck just as a few rain drops sprinkled the windshield. As Joe was driving out, Morgan suddenly told Joe she wanted to talk to the groundskeeper before they left.

"What do you want to talk to him about?" Joe asked.

"Aren't you just a little curious about those flowers?"

"What do you mean?"

"The flowers. Those were fresh flowers. Who put them there?"

"Maybe your mom?"

"No way," Morgan was stressed out from the day and the impatience in her voice was evident. "Yellow, long-stemmed roses? Are you kidding? That was a fifty dollar bouquet, at least. My mother couldn't afford that."

The old man was still hunched over his tractor. He looked up this time when Joe stopped in front of the open garage door. Morgan was first out and Joe followed dutifully.

"Sir, we found the graves," Morgan said. "Thanks. We were wondering about the flowers on the grave of Suda O'Donnell. She is my great-grandmother. Do you happen to know anything about the flowers?"

The old man stood up, pulled a red rag out of a back pocket, and wiped some grease from his hands.

"I just know that somebody sends a check to a local florist with instructions to keep fresh roses on her grave year 'round. That's how I knew about her grave when you said her name."

Joe and Morgan looked at each other. She turned back to the old man.

"Any idea who does this?" she asked, then added to clarify, "who sends the check, I mean?"

"Nope. No idea. I just know that there's been yellow roses delivered to that grave every other day for at least four or five years now."

Now Morgan Sanders and Joe Rocker had a second mystery.

Chapter 26

"So what does your mom think of the diary?" Joe asked Morgan as he pulled his truck into the parking lot of the Red Bank Library.

"She couldn't put it down," Morgan answered. "She read it all in one sitting. She never knew much about her grandparents' early lives, and all that trouble with the Klan—she said her Grandpa Thomas never mentioned anything about that."

The library parking lot was almost full. Joe finally found a space near the back of the lot.

Since the visit to the cemetery, Morgan and Joe had thought often of the mysterious yellow roses delivered to Suda's grave. After he dropped off Morgan that day, Joe drove back to the cemetery and asked the groundskeeper if he knew which florist delivered the flowers. The florist would be able to tell him who ordered and paid for the flowers. Joe thought he was in luck when the groundskeeper told him the name of the florist—a place where Angela Kell, Tim Grainger's girlfriend, worked.

But unfortunately Angela could not help. After checking through the receipts, all she could tell Joe was that the roses were ordered and paid for anonymously through some accounting company. Joe called the company, but was told all information about their clients' business dealings was confidential.

Joe and Morgan's thoughts were on the flowers as they walked toward the library entrance.

"Does your mom have any idea who might be putting flowers on Suda's grave?"

"No clue," Morgan answered as she opened the library door.

"Do you have any hunches?" Joe asked Morgan.

"About the flowers?"

"Yes."

"It's all I've thought about since we visited the cemetery," said Morgan. "The only one from the diary who might still be living is Henry

Niemeier, the little crippled boy."

"I thought of him, too," admitted Joe. "But if it's Henry, why did he just recently start sending the flowers? That old groundskeeper told us the flowers had been coming for four or five years. Why would Henry wait all this time?"

"I don't know," Morgan shrugged. "But who else could it be?"

"Maybe Tommy put something in his will so flowers would be delivered to the grave," Joe offered weakly, knowing there was a major weakness to that theory, which Morgan immediately pointed out.

"Grandpa Thomas—Tommy—died in 1988," Morgan reminded Joe needlessly. "If the groundskeeper is right about how long the flowers have been delivered, then they started coming around 1996 or '97. Why would he put in his will to wait seven or eight years after he died before starting the flower deliveries? It doesn't make sense. Besides, my mother remembers nothing about flowers in Grandpa Thomas's will. Mom said almost all of Grandpa Thomas's estate went to pay off the doctors and hospitals after his long battle with cancer. She said the lawyers got what was left after the medical bills were paid."

"It looks like I have another trip to make to the Willard Library," Joe said, "to see if I can find out what became of Henry Niemeier."

"*We* have a trip to make to Willard Library," Morgan corrected Joe's pronoun.

But Morgan and Joe had two puzzles to solve, and the one concerning the mysterious flowers would have to wait. Their goal today was to see what information they could assemble on the Ku Klux Klan of the 1920's and get a lead on how Tommy's trouble with the Klan, and the law, was resolved. According to Mr. Holden, this library was a good source for background information about the 1920's KKK.

Once inside, Morgan sat down at a reference computer to see what she could bring up about the Klan. Joe spotted Dave Geyer, a former teammate of Joe's who had graduated two years ago and was now attending the University of Southern Indiana. Geyer shared a table with a girl as he looked up and spotted Joe approaching.

"Hey, Joe," Geyer said and raised his hand.

Joe exchanged a high five and kidded his former teammate. "I can see you're pretending to be a college student."

"*Pretending* is a good word for it," Geyer responded. Geyer introduced the blonde girl at his table. *Sharon* was nicely dressed and was clearly a frequent visitor to the tanning salon. Joe nodded and exchanged a greeting with the girl.

"What are you working on?" Joe asked the pair.

"The Ancient Greeks," Geyer shook his head and rolled his eyes. "If you ever attend USI, make sure you never get a professor named Eric Vonfuhrmann. You have to work your butt off to get a 'C.' Nobody warned Sharon and me about him and we were unlucky enough to get him for a humanities class. That's where Sharon and I met. We've been either here or at the USI library every night this week looking up stuff on some hippie named Homer who used to memorize entire books of crazy poetry no one can understand. No one but Vonfuhrmann, anyway. If you ask me, the only Homer we need to know about is Simpson."

Sharon giggled.

"What brings you here, Rocker?" Geyer asked.

"We're trying to find some information on the Ku Klux Klan."

"We?" Geyer commented. He saw no one with Joe.

"I'm with that girl over there." Joe pointed to Morgan who was busy writing down a list of book titles from the computer screen.

Dave Geyer looked at Morgan, then at Joe, then back at Morgan a second time. The pale Morgan Sanders with the jet black frazzled hairdo, clashing makeup, and strange wardrobe was a stark contrast from the blonde, artificially tanned Sharon in her designer jeans and jacket.

"Rocker," Geyer turned to Joe, "if you can't get a date, I'm sure Sharon can introduce you to one of her sorority sisters. You don't have to settle for something the cat dragged in." Geyer thought he was being funny and expected Joe to laugh. Sharon did so.

Joe felt his face flush. "We're not dating. We're here trying to find some information for a history project." Joe felt no need to detail all the specifics.

"That's good news," Geyer responded, "the 'not dating' part, I mean. I was starting to worry about you."

Joe wanted to hear no more and made a hasty exit. Geyer told Joe to stay in touch.

Stay in touch. Yeah right, you jerk. Joe thought as he walked away.

Joe was mad at Dave Geyer but madder at himself, ashamed he had not defended Morgan; instead he made sure Geyer knew he was not dating her. Was he too concerned with his reputation? Mr. Football Hero? For a moment Joe considered returning and giving Geyer an earful, but it was too late. The opportunity to do right had presented itself and he passed it up. He was not proud of himself.

Morgan looked up, spotted Joe, and waved him over.

"Where you been, cowboy?"

"Back there talking to a guy who was on the team a couple of years ago."

Morgan felt Joe's obvious lack of enthusiasm. "Well, I'm glad seeing an old friend perked you up," she joked.

Joe ignored her and changed the subject. "What did you find?"

"I don't have the Internet at home, do you?" Morgan asked Joe.

"Yeah."

"We'll have to use yours at home if we want stuff from the Net. There are hundreds of hit sites about the Klan but, like at school, the library has a nanny on many of them and you can't bring them up." Morgan handed Joe a small piece of paper with the name and call numbers of some books. "I brought up a list of books. Find some of these and see what you think; I'll ask someone about old newspaper articles."

Joe found the non-fiction section and in a minute found two of the books on Morgan's list. One title was *The Fiery Cross: The Ku Klux Klan in America* by a man named Wyn Craig Wade. The other was a compilation of papers entitled *D.C. Stephenson: Irvington 0492.* From the diary, Joe remembered Suda's encounter with this man named Stephenson. Mr. Holden had also mentioned him.

Joe sat at a table and opened the book on Stephenson. A

full-page-sized photograph taken of the man in 1925 was the first thing Joe saw when he opened the book. Well groomed and impeccably dressed in what was obviously an expensive suit, the cherubic-faced Stephenson seemed not the least bit intimidating. His appearance seemed more in line with what one would expect from a doctor or judge than the Grand Dragon of the Ku Klux Klan.

Chapter 27

Football season was over at Reitz High School.

After the nerve-racking win over the Castle Knights in the Sectional Championship Game, the next weekend the team traveled to Bloomington to take on number-one-rated Bloomington South. Dropped passes, one to a wide open receiver in the endzone, doomed the Reitz Panthers who put up another inspired defensive effort. But when the gun sounded, the Panthers were on the short end of a 13 to 8 score. Many sports reporters and close followers of Indiana high school football felt the two best teams in the state played in that game. Newspapers the next day claimed that the state championship had now been decided, even though semi-state and state championship games were still to be played. Indeed, Bloomington South would go on to win the 5A state championship, blowing out their remaining opponents.

It took Joe several days to accept the fact that his days of playing football for Reitz were over. He spoke little at home or school for three or four days. But he had always known that it would end someday. A consolation that helped Joe out of his doldrums was that he had no personal regrets about how hard he had worked during his years in the football program. In the past, he had occasionally heard seniors—after their last game—lamenting the fact that perhaps they could have done more: *"I wish I would have worked harder in the weightroom during the offseason, I could have been All-City"* or *"I wish I would have worked harder on my speed."* At least these regrets did not haunt Joe. He knew he had worked as hard as possible to make himself the best player he could be, doing everything the coaches asked and more. Joe would run extra Bowl steps after practice if he felt he needed the extra conditioning, and he never faked a hard workout in the weightroom as he had seen some players do. He always went all out in the weightroom.

Joe felt he had done things the right way. This thought helped him adjust to the end of high school football. Life goes on. College coaches had begun calling early in the season, and now he had some recruiting visits to make.

As Joe walked to class, he heard Morgan call out behind him.

"Joe."

Joe stopped, turned, and waited for her to catch up.

"How's my favorite linebacker? Are you okay?"

"Yeah, I'm okay."

"I know losing that game has to be rough," Morgan said as they began walking.

Joe was silent.

"I made a trip to Willard Library last night," Morgan announced.

"What for?" Joe asked, then he remembered. "Oh . . . Henry Niemeier I bet."

"That's right. I don't think Henry has anything to do with the flowers, but I still wanted to know what happened to him."

"So, what did you find?"

"Henry died in 1991 at the age of seventy-five," Morgan said.

"Did he live in Evansville his whole life?"

"Don't know, but he died here. I have the address listed on the death certificate. It's somewhere on Missouri Street. There is a next of kin listed at that address. It was only eleven years ago that Henry died. Maybe the relative still lives there and can tell us something about the old days."

"Missouri Street, that's on the north side of town," Joe said. "When are we going?"

"After school today."

"What was the house number again?" Joe asked Morgan as he turned his truck left off Columbia Avenue and onto Main Street.

Morgan repeated the address on Missouri Street.

"That will be just a couple of blocks east of Main," Joe said.

Joe turned right onto Missouri, drove a couple of blocks, then spotted the house number on his left. This was an older neighborhood, made up of older frame homes with small yards. Few of the houses had driveways, so cars lined both sides of the narrow street. Joe drove to the end of the block, turned the truck around, then drove back and parked by the curb in front of the house. Joe and Morgan crossed a small yard, climbed three concrete steps to a wooden porch, and rang the doorbell. They waited, pushed the button again, and were about to leave when the door opened. An elderly lady in a flowered dress and pink apron stood in the doorway.

"Hello, ma'am," Morgan said.

"Hello." The lady returned the greeting.

"You don't know us. My name is Morgan Sanders and this is Joe Rocker. We are trying to find some information on someone who used to live at this address."

"Who is that?" the lady asked.

"A man named Henry Niemeier. He apparently lived here when he passed away about eleven years ago."

The old lady looked at Morgan, then at Joe, then back at Morgan. "What do you want to know about Henry?"

"So you know him?" Morgan's excitement was evident.

"Henry was my cousin. He lived here for the last twenty years of his life. My husband and I took care of Henry, then after my husband passed it was just Henry and me."

"Could we ask you a few questions, ma'am?" Morgan asked.

The woman paused again and looked at the two young people. "Come in." She opened the door and stepped aside.

The woman led Morgan and Joe into the living room and offered them a seat. She excused herself and left the room, returning shortly with a small plate of cookies. She set the plate on a coffee table in front of Morgan and Joe.

The old woman's name was Mrs. Schneider. She told them that her mother was the only sister of Henry's mother, making Mrs. Schneider and Henry first cousins. Morgan took her turn and satisfied the old woman's curiosity about why they sought information on Henry. She told Mrs. Schneider about Joe finding an old diary from the 1920s that mentions Henry as a small boy.

"Whose diary was it?" Mrs. Schneider asked.

"Suda O'Donnell; her maiden name was Jackson. Suda was my great-grandmother."

The old woman looked at Morgan. "I thought you looked familiar."

"You knew my great-grandmother?"

"No, not personally. I never met her, but I feel like I know her from listening to Henry talk of her over the years. He kept a picture of her on the wall in his room. It hung there for years. I normally never let strangers in, but when I answered the door, I thought I knew you from somewhere. Now I know where. You look a lot like the girl in the picture."

"Do you still have that picture?"

"Yes. It's packed away in a box with the rest of Henry's belongings. Poor Henry didn't leave much behind. He was crippled, you know. He used to volunteer two days a week down at the Goodwill, but besides that he didn't get out much. And Henry never cared much about material things. Family and friends were all that mattered to Henry."

Joe had gobbled down all the cookies so Mrs. Schneider asked if he wanted more.

"Yes, thanks," he said as he swallowed the last bite. Morgan looked at him and turned back to Mrs. Schneider shaking her head. The old lady laughed.

"If you'll follow me, young man, I'll let you bring out the box with Henry's belongings. You two are welcome to look through it. I'll get more cookies."

Joe followed Mrs. Schneider out of the room, and in a few minutes he returned with a cardboard box with the name *Henry* written large at both ends. Joe set the box on the coffee table. It was large box but not heavy. Inside were the few material things that Henry Niemeier had deemed important enough to keep during his lifetime. There were several pictures of Henry's mother and some of other family members. An ancient scrapbook held sepia photographs and a couple of yellowed newspaper articles detailing Tommy O'Donnell's exploits on the Reitz gridiron. Also inside the box was an old football that would never again hold air. The football was signed "To Henry from Tommy."

Then Morgan spotted the photograph that Mrs. Schneider had told them about. It was in a metal frame not unlike the wedding photo of Suda and Tommy that Morgan had come across at home. This picture had also been taken at Suda and Tommy's wedding. A young man in suit and tie who looked to be thirteen or fourteen years of age sat in a wheelchair between the bride and groom. The boy in the wheelchair—Henry, of course—blushed and smiled broadly as Suda hugged him and kissed him on the cheek. Another photo, also framed, pictured just Suda and Tommy.

"Unbelievable," Joe said as he stared at the photographs. "It's like history coming to life before your eyes."

Morgan too stared at the photos and the face of the bride who could have been her twin. Joe looked at her.

"It's a little spooky how much you two look alike," he said. Morgan ignored him and continued to gaze at her face in the photographs.

Joe rummaged through the rest of the contents. There were keepsakes not as old. Henry had apparently developed an interest in chess. A small box contained a chessboard, pieces, and a book on chess strategy. He also collected headlines from important days in history. A yellowed and torn front page from the *Evansville Courier* dated December 8, 1941, announced the previous day's attack on Pearl Harbor. There were front pages proclaiming D-Day, VE day, the death of Franklin Roosevelt, VJ day, the assassination of JFK, and the moon landing in 1969. Joe was careful not to tear the fragile paper.

Morgan continued to gaze at the photographs, almost entranced. As Joe returned the newspaper clippings and the chess board to the box, he noticed what looked like a small shoe box that had been buried under the other items. Joe lifted the box and removed the lid. Inside were more yellowed papers but not from a newspaper. The words on the pages were handwritten and Joe recognized the handwriting. It struck him like a thunderbolt.

Here were the missing pages of Suda Mae Jackson's diary.

Chapter 28

"Unbelievable," Joe said. "Your great-grandmother was really something."

Morgan just nodded as she looked over an affidavit that had been among the missing pages of Suda's diary. From the diary's missing pages, the mystery of the disappearance of Hubert Jenkins—the man Tommy O'Donnell was accused of murdering—was finally solved.

After sneaking out of the house after Mrs. Pampe had fallen asleep, Suda had spent several uneventful nights watching the KKK headquarters on Edgar Street. In her diary she mentioned she was not sure exactly what she hoped to find out from her spying, but there she was, in her coat, standing in the shadows in the alley behind the building. This went on for several nights.

Being early December the windows were closed, so Suda had no hopes of skulking up closer to the house and listening to conversations inside. But D.C. Stephenson frowned on smoking so when members wanted a cigarette they were forced to congregate on the back porch. It was during one of these back porch pow wows when Suda heard Hubert Jenkins' name mentioned. And funny thing, the name was not mentioned in a past tense as one would expect of a deceased person. Present tense was used.

The newspaper had published Jenkins' home address when it reported his disappearance. Suda had saved that newspaper article and the next night she carefully approached a house on Read Street. Suda tried to get close enough to look in windows, but a large and very loud dog in the backyard began barking when it saw her and, even though she was at the side of the house and not in the yard with the dog, she had to leave quickly.

Suda returned the next night with several pieces of leftover fried chicken. The meat quieted the dog while Suda peered in windows. After spotting nothing on the main floor, she checked two basement windows that had been covered on the inside with black paper. The blackout was sloppily done. One window supplied a half inch gap that the paper failed to cover, and through that window Suda saw five men sitting around a table playing cards. And low and behold if one of the men was not Hubert Jenkins!

The diary told the whole story.

Suda summoned Tommy from his aunt's farm in Illinois and returned to the house on Read Street two nights later, luckily finding Jenkins home alone. Suda threw a brick through the basement window (apparently the dim-witted Jenkins considered his basement with its poorly blacked out windows a sufficient hiding place). After breaking the window, Suda called Jenkins a bad name (*another confession for me,* Suda wrote in her diary) and challenged him to come out front and fight a girl. Jenkins, more than anxious to settle accounts with the person who had broken his nose, even if it was a girl, took the bait. Jenkins bolted out the front door only to be waylaid by Tommy O'Donnell, who with one punch broke his nose again and knocked him unconscious.

Tommy slung the coo cooed Jenkins over his shoulder and loaded him in his aunt's Model T. Not comfortable with simply turning Jenkins over to the police, many of whom had ties to or political sympathies toward the Klan, Suda had made an arrangement with a local photographer. They drove to the photographer's house who took a photograph of the hapless Hubert Jenkins sitting with eyes open but only half conscious with a ballooned nose and a silly grin on his face.

Suda held the front page of that day's newspaper to Jenkins' chest to prove when the photograph was taken. The photographer was a fellow parishioner at Saint Boniface, and he promised to develop the picture that night. While Tommy returned the still groggy Hubert Jenkins to his house on Read Street, depositing him without fanfare on the walk in front of the house, Suda waited for the negative to be developed. Finally, the photographer handed over several copies of the photograph, refusing any payment.

The diary went on to tell, in Suda's colorful way, of the next day when Suda and Tommy made a fateful call on D.C. Stephenson at the Klan headquarters on Edgar Street. Stephenson made no comment when told that Suda had found Jenkins at home, but his face betrayed his incredulity at the stupidity of his underling (Stephenson had ordered Jenkins to leave town).

Suda had Stephenson and the Klan over a barrel. The Klan prided itself on, and used as a main tenet of its creed, a zealous support of the law. If their scheme to falsely accuse an innocent man of murder became known, it could deal a severe blow to both the Klan's standing in the community and recruitment efforts. The Grand Dragon had no choice but to sign Suda's affidavit admitting the Klan's culpability and agree to produce Hubert Jenkins to the public. The Klan would be allowed to inform the police that the accusations against Tommy O'Donnell had been a regrettable mistake brought about by witnesses jumping to conclusions. Suda also demanded that the Ku Klux Klan stop the harassment of Catholics immediately. In return, Suda agreed to never make the real facts public—unless, of course, Stephenson broke his end of the bargain.

It was all there in the missing pages of the diary: the story, the paper signed by D.C. Stephenson, a copy of the photograph of Hubert Jenkins, and even the reason the pages were torn from the diary. Fearing the Klan might break into Mrs. Pampe's home and search for the documents, Suda removed the last part of her diary and gave it to Henry Niemeier for safekeeping.

And the papers stayed in Henry's belongings for eighty-one years—until the day Suda's great-granddaughter called on Henry's cousin.

Chapter 29

[four months later]

"The waltz will begin in five minutes! The waltz will begin in five minutes!"

The anonymous voice piped from the public address system at the Scottish Rite Temple. It was the night of the Reitz High prom, easily evidenced by young ladies in beautiful gowns and young men in dapper tuxedos.

Around one table sat Rick Turner and his date, Becky Taylor. Tim Grainger accompanied his girlfriend, Angela Kell. One other couple sat with them—Joe Rocker and Morgan Sanders.

Joe had asked Morgan to the prom a couple of months ago. Morgan at first said no. She had always made fun of proms, calling them "bourgeois."

She could not explain to herself why, but she called Joe later that night and told him she changed her mind.

Neither partner was very sure of their choice: Joe for asking, and Morgan for accepting. But here they were, Morgan with hair and makeup nicely done and wearing a strapless burgundy sheath. Her nose ring was gone. She looked lovely and Joe wished Dave Geyer could see Morgan now. For his part, Joe was quite dapper in a black tux.

Morgan was a junior and only seniors could waltz, so Morgan and Joe remained at the table while the two other couples took their places on the dance floor. The music began and the couples waltzed around the perimeter of the dance floor. The scene reminded Joe of a Scarlet Pimpernel movie.

When the waltz ended, the evening reverted to normal prom mode: couples sat at tables or circulated throughout the room visiting with friends; a DJ played the latest rock 'n roll and rap favorites while many couples danced. Chaperones, mostly teachers from the school, filled drink cups and replenished pretzel bowls.

Alone at the table, Joe and Morgan talked about the diary and their adventure last fall.

"I wonder if Suda and Tommy ever went dancing," Joe wondered.

"Oh, I'm sure they did," Morgan said confidently. "Certainly they would have danced at their wedding."

Joe nodded.

Joe and Morgan had not spent much time together since they solved the diary's mystery. They talked if they saw each other in the hallway at school, and a couple of times they sat together and talked during lunch, but even that was a couple of months ago. They used some time to catch up.

"I saw in the newspaper a while back that you're going to SIU (Joe had signed on to play football for Southern Illinois University). I bet you're pretty excited about that."

"You bet! They offered me a full ride—tuition, books, room and board, all paid for. Other schools recruited me but some offered only partial scholarships. So now I'm a Saluki."

"A what?" Morgan asked.

"A Saluki."

"What's that."

"It's an Egyptian dog, kind of like a greyhound. They say it's the world's oldest purebred dog."

"Oh."

"SIU is in Carbondale, Illinois," Joe added. "That's where Tommy went when he had to leave town for a while, remember?"

"Yes, I remember."

"It's only a couple of hours drive to Carbondale. Close enough I can get home on weekends after football season. Maybe you can make it over for a game sometime, since you never saw me play for Reitz."

"Who says I didn't?" Morgan smiled.

"You did. You told me you never attended a game."

"I told a fib. I was at the Castle game."

"What? But you said. . . ."

"Like I said, I lied."

After a slight pause in the conversation, Joe asked Morgan about her plans.

"I'm not sure," Morgan said. "I still have a year to decided." Morgan knew the money for college would be tough to come by.

Joe asked Morgan if she wanted to dance. She rose and they found a spot on the crowded dance floor.

After the dance, Joe and Morgan stood under a flowered trellis and posed for the official prom photo.

Time flew. More conversation was followed by dancing until almost midnight. Rick and Becky went on the hunt for something to eat when it was time to leave the prom. Tim, Angela, Joe, and Morgan decided on bowling at Arc Lanes.

Morgan had never bowled, but she had her great-grandmother's stubbornness for trying and, after a few pointers from Joe, she was not doing badly for a first-timer.

As they bowled, Morgan remembered Joe telling her that Angela worked at the flower shop that furnished the flowers for Suda's grave. Even though the missing diary pages had revealed the resolution to the KKK plot against Tommy, still there was the mystery of the yellow roses delivered every other day to Suda's grave. Morgan visited the grave often (once, as she arrived, she saw Joe driving away). The fresh roses were always there.

"Joe tells me you work at the flower shop that delivers flowers to my great-grandmother's grave," Morgan said to Angela as they sat and waited on the guys to bowl.

"Yeah. Joe told me that you two were really curious about who pays for the flowers. I tried to find out, but everything is handled anonymously through an accounting service."

"So there is no way to find out?"

"I don't know how. Only a couple of checks come a year, made out for enough to cover six months. We don't even see the checks at the store. They are mailed directly to our bookkeeper. All we see at the store is the order, and it's just a handwritten piece of paper from our manager. In fact, since we do it every other day, he doesn't even bother writing out an order anymore."

Joe and Tim were both good bowlers and they were not shy about letting everyone know it. Joe threw a strike and let out a whoop.

"I'm so good sometimes I scare myself," Joe said as he sat down with the girls. He took a huge gulp of his Coke.

"Of course you are," Morgan told him, "because you're a big strong man."

Joe nodded his head in agreement and felt the muscle in his right arm. "At least she's observant," he said to Angela.

Both girls looked at each other and rolled their eyes.

Tim finished a spare then joined the others.

"How 'bout after this game we split and go after a pizza," Tim suggested.

Joe looked at his watch. "I promised Morgan's mother I'd have her home by two-thirty." It was now almost two.

When they finished the game, Joe and Morgan said good night to Tim and Angela and walked out the door of the bowling alley into a pouring rain. Joe sprinted to his car; he had rented a Ford Mustang convertible for the prom. Unfortunately the top would have to stay up. By the time they were in the car, they were both soaked. They laughed at each other's wet clothes.

"Maybe they'll give you a partial refund for washing your tuxedo before you return it," Morgan laughed.

"As long as they don't fine me for returning it three sizes smaller when it shrinks."

They laughed together.

Wipers on high barely kept up with the downpour as Joe turned onto Maryland Street. Luckily he found a place to pull over directly in front of Morgan's apartment building.

He turned off the engine.

"I never thought I would ever attend a prom," Morgan said, "and I worried about how this night would work out. But I had fun tonight.

Thanks for asking me, Joe."

"I had a good time too. I'm glad we were together. We haven't spent as much time together the past few months." Joe paused. "I missed you."

Morgan looked at Joe but did not speak. A relief to Joe, who surprised himself at what he had said.

"Well," Joe said. "It's two-thirty. I better get you to your door."

Joe got out, circled around the car, and opened the door for Morgan. Through the rain they sprinted to the building and the cover of the doorway entrance.

"Hey, you're pretty fast for a girl." They paused for a moment then laughed together as they remembered Suda making that claim.

"Well, thanks again, Joe. Good night." Morgan turned to walk into the building. Joe turned toward the street.

"Joe."

Joe turned. Two dripping wet teenagers kissed.

Chapter 30

"Joe."

No answer. Joe's father stood at the bottom of the stairs.

"Joe! Telephone!"

Upstairs, Joe had dozed off while watching the Food Channel. Apparently Joe's mind sought another realm when Emeril started cooking duck burritos. His father's third yell woke him.

"Joe!"

"Yeah, Dad!"

"Telephone! And your mom says dinner will be ready in ten minutes!"

"Okay!" Joe picked up the receiver. "Got it, Dad!"

"Hello."

"Hello, Joe?" It was a girl's voice.

"Yes."

"Hi, Joe, this is Angela."

"Hey, Angela. What's up?"

"I know you and Morgan are curious about who sends the flowers for Morgan's grandmother's grave."

"Great-grandmother," Joe corrected pleasantly. "Why, did you find out?" He was fully awake now and all ears. Angela worked at the flower shop that delivered the roses.

"No, I don't have a name. But the arrangers—that's what I do—got a note from the manager today telling us not to have the flowers delivered to that grave on Monday. I asked the manager why. He said his bookkeeper called to tell him a representative of the person who sends the flowers called to inform him that his client—the person responsible for sending the flowers—will deliver them personally on Memorial Day."

"Memorial Day?" Joe was just making sure.

"Yeah, that's this coming Monday."

"Right. Thanks, Angela."

"Sorry I couldn't come up with a name. I not sure even our bookkeeper knows it."

"That's okay, Angela. I really appreciate this. Thanks."

"You're welcome. Bye, Joe."

"Bye."

Joe dialed Morgan's phone number.

Chapter 31

Morgan and Joe knew it would likely be a long Memorial Day stakeout at Saint Joseph Cemetery. They had no idea what time the mysterious "flower person" would arrive, so by 8:00 a.m. they were sitting on a heavy metal bench a couple of hundred feet away from Suda's and Tommy's graves. They had decided to position themselves away from the graves just in case the mystery man—or woman—proved shy. On the way to the cemetery that morning, Joe stopped at McDonald's. As they sat on the bench, he finished off his two breakfast burritos, a sausage egg McMuffin, and three hash brown patties. Joe crumpled up the trash and tossed it into a metal trash container near the bench.

"I'm still hungry," Joe said. "I should have gotten some hotcakes."

Morgan looked at him and shook her head. "How can you eat like that?"

"Like what?" Joe took the lid off of his large orange juice and took several long gulps.

"Never mind."

When Joe picked up Morgan that morning, she was carrying a shoulder bag. He had never seen Morgan with a purse or any type of tote bag.

"What's in that bag?" he asked.

"Why, are you writing a book?"

It seemed appropriate to just sit and listen. Memorial Day visitors would start arriving soon, but for now Morgan and Joe were alone. The stand of trees that stood sentinel behind their bench supplied not only shade for two young people but a stage for the choir of birds offering their morning recital. The temperature was perfect and the sky as blue as Elvis's shoes.

"How's it feel to be a high school graduate?" Morgan asked. Seniors, like Joe, had walked the walk last Wednesday. Morgan would be a senior next fall.

"Feels great. I liked high school okay, but I'm ready to move on." Joe had his work cut out for him this summer. His college football coaches had sent him a rigorous summer conditioning program.

The earlier hours passed. Sitting forced both Morgan and Joe to occasionally stretch their legs. They took short walks, sometimes together, other times separately, but never out of sight of Suda's and Tommy's graves. By ten o'clock others wandered through the plots, placing flowers and paying respects. Some paused for only a moment. Others lingered. Not far from where Morgan and Joe sat, an elderly lady stood talking to the headstone of a husband lost years ago. Farther away, a couple in their mid-30s looked sadly at the resting place of a young child. Others came and went. Occasionally someone would walk by Suda's grave, drawing Morgan and Joe's attention, but no one stopped.

As noon approached, Joe decided to get lunch while Morgan stayed behind to keep the vigil. He returned twenty minutes later with Subway sandwiches and soft drinks. They finished lunch, took a walk, sat for awhile, then walked some more. Afternoon hours ticked away. Three o'clock arrived and still there had been no visitor to Suda's grave.

"What if he, or she, doesn't show?" Joe asked Morgan.

"He'll show."

Joe looked at her but said no more.

At half past four, Morgan walked down to the restrooms, a five minute walk away. Joe, extremely tired of the bench, laid on his side in the grass. The air was warm, the grass cool, and Joe's eyelids grew heavy. When the big limousine arrived, he might have been asleep had it not been for a crying baby in a stroller a few rows down the hill.

At first Joe ignored the car as it drove slowly up the road. After all, big black limousines were not uncommon in cemeteries. But this was no funeral procession. The limousine had no escorting cars and the driver maneuvered up the road slowly and deliberately, like a driver in an unfamiliar neighborhood checking for an address.

The limousine stopped several rows down the hill, then moved forward and stopped again. A long moment passed before the driver's door opened and the driver stepped out. Joe watched as the man circled around the vehicle and opened the rear passenger door. Slowly, an old man emerged from the limo and, aided by a cane and escorted by the driver, made his way onto the grass and through the rows of graves, reading names on headstones.

Searching.

The old man carried a bouquet of yellow roses and was finely dressed. His three piece pin-striped suit, obviously custom tailored and expensive, and a fine trilby hat gave the impression that this was a man familiar with wealth. Joe sat up when the old man stopped in front of Suda's grave, stood for a moment, then respectfully removed his hat.

Where the heck is Morgan? Joe stood and looked toward the building Morgan had walked down to but there was no sign of her. Worried the old man might leave before Morgan returned, Joe started toward Suda's grave.

As he approached the old man, Joe felt extremely curious but at the same time quite nervous. Who was behind the mystery of the flowers? And why had he started sending them? The driver stood several yards away, respectfully giving the old man some space. Still holding the flowers, the old man leaned on his cane and stared at Suda's headstone. When Joe reached the grave, he positioned himself six feet, or maybe seven, from the old man who continued to stare at Suda's headstone, oblivious to Joe. Deep in thought, the old man seemed lost in another time and place.

"Hello, sir," Joe said cautiously.

The old man seemed hesitant to take his eyes off of the headstone, but finally he turned and looked at Joe.

"Hello, young man." The old man turned back to the headstone and his thoughts.

Joe wasn't quite sure what to say so he got right to the point. "Did you know Suda?"

Hearing Suda's name spoken out loud seemed to brighten the old man's spirits, and he turned his attention to Joe immediately this time.

"Yes, I knew her," he said proudly and with great reverence. "We were together for only a few days then I never saw her again. Suda was very kind to me and I've never forgotten her. It's been over eighty years, but I remember her face as clearly as if I had seen her just yesterday." Then, realizing the young man questioning him about Suda must have some connection to her, the old man asked a question of his own: "Are you a relative of Suda's?"

"No. I found her diary when my dad and I remodeled an old house."

"A diary?"

"Yes, sir."

Silence followed. Again Joe turned to look for Morgan. He finally spotted her. She was a hundred yards away and running toward them. As she neared, she slowed and came to a stop beside Joe.

The old man appeared stunned as he looked at Morgan.

"Suda," the old man said as if in a dream.

Morgan walked over to the old man and took his hand. "I'm Suda's great-granddaughter. My name's Morgan. This is my friend, Joe Rocker." The old man nodded politely at Joe then returned his gaze to Morgan.

"Suda's great-granddaughter?" A tear ran down the old man's cheek.

Morgan paused for a moment then said, "I see you are finally talking."

The old man smiled.

"She always knew you would make something of yourself," Morgan said.

"The family that adopted me was quite wealthy," said the old man as if he were talking to Suda. "They owned a string of lumber yards in northern Illinois. After college, I entered the family business then took over when my adoptive father died. Now I've handed it over to my son."

"So how did you find where my great-grandmother is buried?"

"I never forgot Suda," the old man said. "A few years ago, when I knew my time was getting short, I hired a private detective to find out where she was and what happened to her." The old man paused and swallowed hard. "It broke my heart to find out she died so young."

"That's when you started sending the flowers." Morgan stated.

The old man nodded.

Morgan looked at Joe who stood silently. Both knew it was time to leave. Morgan took Joe's hand and led him away. As they passed the driver, Morgan opened her tote bag and handed him copies of the pages of Suda's diary, and a copy of Suda and Tommy's wedding photograph.

"How did you know it was him?" Joe asked Morgan as they walked away.

"I just knew."

When they reached Joe's pickup at the bottom of the hill, they looked back at Donald Malcolm McGennis laying flowers on Suda's grave.

About the Author

A native of Denver, Mike Whicker now resides in the Midwest.

The author donates his royalties from the sales
of *Proper Suda* to charity.

Author can be emailed at mike@mikewhicker.com.

Website: www.mikewhicker.com

Other novels by Mike Whicker

Invitation to Valhalla

Blood of the Reich

CPSIA information can be obtained at www.ICGtesting.com
Printed in the USA
LVOW062350261212

313225LV00003B/742/P